Advance Prai

LOVE THE
SINNER

"Lynn Bulock has a talent for combining a fun puzzle
with a heartwarming cast of characters for
a can't-put-down read. I look forward to more!"
—Hannah Alexander, Christy Award-winning author
of *Hideaway* and *Safe Haven*

"Lynn Bulock writes with the kind of smart style
that makes readers feel like the story is unfolding
right before their eyes—and they can't wait
to know what happens next!"
—Annie Jones, award-winning author of *Sadie-in-Waiting*

"*Love the Sinner*, with its down-to-earth
spiritual insights and spunky heroine, will please
many fans of the gentle domestic mystery.
Readers will follow with interest Gracie Lee's search
into the secrets of her husband's mysterious past
and then cheer when she finally discovers the truth.
A welcome addition to the cozy mystery genre."
—Earlene Fowler, author of *Broken Dishes*
and *Delectable Mountains*

To Joe, my very-much-alive hero and husband.
You're my one and only.

LYNN BULOCK

LOVE THE SINNER

Steeple
Hill
Café™

Published by Steeple Hill Books™

If you purchased this book without a cover you should be aware that this book is stolen property. It was reported as "unsold and destroyed" to the publisher, and neither the author nor the publisher has received any payment for this "stripped book."

STEEPLE HILL BOOKS

ISBN 0-373-78539-9

LOVE THE SINNER

Copyright © 2005 by Lynn Bulock

All rights reserved. Except for use in any review, the reproduction or utilization of this work in whole or in part in any form by any electronic, mechanical or other means, now known or hereafter invented, including xerography, photocopying and recording, or in any information storage or retrieval system, is forbidden without the written permission of the editorial office, Steeple Hill Books, 233 Broadway, New York, NY 10279 U.S.A.

All characters in this book have no existence outside the imagination of the author and have no relation whatsoever to anyone bearing the same name or names. They are not even distantly inspired by any individual known or unknown to the author, and all incidents are pure invention.

This edition published by arrangement with Steeple Hill Books.

® and TM are trademarks of Steeple Hill Books, used under license. Trademarks indicated with ® are registered in the United States Patent and Trademark Office, the Canadian Trade Marks Office and in other countries.

www.SteepleHill.com

Printed in U.S.A.

ACKNOWLEDGMENTS

I am indebted to so many people
in the creation of this book and the set of characters
within. My thanks to Dr. D. P. Lyle and Eileen Dreyer, my
dynamite agent, Nancy Yost, and the always-encouraging
enthusiasm of my editor, Diane Dietz. And always, last
but not least, the Princesses of Quite a Lot, who keep me
going with prayer and writing advice when things get
tough: Sharon Gillenwater, Annie Jones and Diane Noble.

For it is by grace you have been saved, through faith—
and this is not from yourselves, it is the gift of God—
not by works, so that no one can boast.

—Ephesians 2:8-9

First, I want to go on record as saying that I, Gracie Lee Harris, did not kill my husband, Dennis Peete. When he died I still thought he was my loving husband, and I had no desire to kill him. That mostly came later. Now if you put me under oath in a court of law and asked me to swear I'd never thought about killing his *mother*, that would be another story. I've thought about that plenty, but nobody's going to come get me on that one.

To the best of my knowledge I've never killed anybody...yet. Even when my first husband, the charming Mr. Harris, dragged me through a divorce I didn't want, and left me with a two-year-old son, I didn't commit murder. I even kept his name so that it would be less confusing for Ben. When it comes to murder, everybody has fantasies, I suspect. But I usually aim mine in other directions. And lately there's been so much going on in real life, who has time for fantasies?

Even so, I'm usually pretty good in a crisis. Everybody has strong points and that's one of mine. So it took a long time for the big, disastrous things in my life to boot me over the edge this time. Maybe it was just taking a chance on love, or life—or whatever—that tilted the balance. If so, that's too bad, because I'm not likely to stop taking chances.

The chances I took earlier in life usually worked out well. The ones I've taken in my relationship with Dennis Peete have been bad news. People who take chances around Dennis don't always fare so well.

Goodness knows I haven't, even before he died. I took a chance on marrying him, and then later another chance nine months ago and sold my condo in Missouri, quit my job and picked up stakes to move out here to California with him, even though he advised against it.

So far, my time here in beautiful downtown Rancho Conejo (and yes, if you speak Spanish, the town is named Rabbit Ranch) has been one big chance after another. Many of those chances have involved the roller-coaster ride of living with my mother-in-law, which I thought would work out just fine even though Dennis thought otherwise.

At the time I thought some of his arguments against our shared living arrangement were almost sweet. Part of the reason he didn't want me out here was that he was pouring all his—and my—money into his franchise business, and living with his mother to save on rent. Silly me. I decided if he was willing to take that chance, I was too. Now I wonder. Who knows? If it weren't for my taking chances, maybe Dennis would still be alive.

* * *

No, I can't fault myself for taking chances. The first big chance I took threw me straight back into the arms of Jesus, clinging to the little bits of sanity that still exist in my disordered life. Without taking chances, my life wouldn't be worth much.

The biggest chance lately came while I was wandering through the college bookstore at Pacific Oaks Christian College, picking up books and putting them back during the first week of this semester. By the end of January when my second semester of grad school started, Dennis had been out of work and in a coma at Conejo Care for four months. Money was tight and I was dithering about how many of these hideously expensive textbooks I could actually afford.

For about the hundredth time, I was wishing Dennis had shared a little more information about business while he still had the chance. The $30k from the sale of my condo could have gone a long way toward this new education I'd committed to before his car accident. I'd done my best trying to find it in his investments, but so far was having precious little luck.

So there I am, walking up and down the psychology and education stacks in the campus bookstore when the dam finally bursts. Like I said before, I'm good in a crisis. I do not lose it in public. This time, however, was different. Juggling a pile of outrageously expensive books, taking one off the stack I carried only to be faced with putting another one back, finally put me in tears. Add that to the fact that what I could afford in the way of school supplies made a pile I should have had a cart for, but kept dropping instead, and you can see the lovely picture I presented.

Then somebody came up behind me and a voice said, "You look like you could use some help."

It was a nice voice, so I didn't immediately turn, snarling, and bite her head off, which was my first impulse. "Oh, no. Does it show that badly?" I asked. My voice sounded wavery even to me as I turned around. The tears really started in earnest then, and I was afraid I was going to do one of those awful heaving sob things, like toddlers do when they're too tired.

"Well, I was talking about the books," the stranger said, holding out a handled basket. "But yeah, now that you mention it…"

Two minutes later the bookstore's assistant manager, Linnette Parks, was my new best friend. "She has the decaf. I've got the real thing," she directed the teenaged waitress at the Coffee Corner, the shop adjoining the bookstore, who came to the table bearing two foaming lattes.

"Now let me get this straight," she said, handing me a napkin out of the tabletop dispenser. I was still a bit of a mess. "You're living with your mother-in-law. Alone."

"Since Dennis's accident. About five months ago."

"From what you've said so far, she sounds like a harridan."

I shrugged. "Maybe that's a little harsh. Without Dennis to referee, our life together has been kind of grim at times. He could manage his mother—Edna thinks he walks on water. I'm just the horrible woman who stole him away and made him stay in Missouri for years longer than he should have, according to her."

"And before the accident, he was traveling a lot?"

"From the day I moved out here. And before I could even harp on that properly like a normal wife, he had a terrible accident that put him in the hospital, and then into one of those places euphemistically called 'long-term care.'"

Linnette looked at me over her latte. "What are the prospects of him recovering?"

I used my napkin again before I answered. "They've never been good. Although Edna is positive he's just going to sit up and start chatting with her one day." I would have argued against that, but Edna doesn't listen to me. This conversation was so odd. Normally I'm the one doing the listening, not the talking in these situations. One major thing I've noticed is that in California total strangers will share information with you that I would have, in Missouri, put on a "need-to-know" basis with my best friend. Maybe it's because everybody and their golden retriever have a shrink out here. Or maybe the sunshine gets to your brain. Whatever the case, I have never learned so much about so many people by merely standing in line at the grocery store or the library.

My mother would say it's not just Californians, it's that invisible sign on my forehead. The one that seems to say You Can Talk To Gracie Lee About Anything And She'll Listen. I'm telling you, it's there. And it's tattooed in special ink. All the folks who receive radio signals from Jupiter through the walls of their apartment can see it. So why not Californians? A lot of them can tune in Jupiter without even putting tinfoil on their TV antennae.

This time around I'd seemed to find that rare kindred spirit with the same I Listen tattoo. The craziest part of the whole thing was that even as I sat there sniffling and talking to Linnette, I had the weird urge to ask her where she got her hair done. She had gorgeous red waves, the kind you don't get from a drugstore tint. Everybody out here does something to their hair and my mousy natural brown, curly or not, suffers in comparison.

Midwestern sense kept me silent on the hair thing. I just took another sip of my latte and tried to calm down. "And you're managing all of this okay?"

"Well, other than losing it occasionally in a bookstore. And if you really want to know, that's not all that's nuts about my life."

"Let me guess. You have teenagers." Linnette's wan smile said she had to be a kindred spirit.

"One. Ben's seventeen and I left him back in Missouri living with his grandmother so he can finish his senior year. I've been raising him alone since his father and I divorced, which was back when dinosaurs roamed the earth. So Ben is as easy as dealing with teen males ever gets. Mostly I'd have to say that living with Edna with no referee is what has me losing it."

Linnette was giving me a real thoughtful look. Finally she drank some of her own coffee and put it down. "I don't usually do this with total strangers," she began, starting a little wave of panic in me.

In Missouri something slightly daring but relatively sane would have followed that phrase. Here in sunny California, she might be offering me anything from acupuncture to EST therapy to things beyond my imagination. Fortunately for me, as I found out later, Linnette was born in Michigan. "Would you think I was too forward if I asked you to come to my church? Not just to attend services, although we want to have you there, too, but to this group we have. It's called Christian Friends, and I think maybe you'd get something out of it."

I'd heard of them before. They weren't just some odd California thing, but had come out of my stomping grounds in the middle of the country and spread all over. "Where's your church? And when's the group thing?" I didn't have enough time to do much, with classes starting up again and my daily visits to the Conejo Board and Care to sit with my comatose husband.

"Conejo Community Chapel, right here in Rancho Conejo," she said. "And my particular Christian Friends group meets twice a month at seven-thirty on Wednesday nights. We're meeting next week if you can hang on that long."

"I think I can. And that would fit into my schedule so I wouldn't have to miss class."

Linnette had a nice smile. "Great. If you come I won't feel quite so guilty about accosting a total stranger. Let me go into the back room of the bookstore and get my purse. It's got a Friends flyer in it that even has a decent map of how to get to the chapel."

She was gone and back again before I could chicken out. The brochure was nice. It described a caring, Christian circle of "praying friends to get you through life's hard spots." Okay, so maybe it was a little too much happy talk, but that was okay. I could use the friends right now, and prayer is never a bad thing.

I got a hug from my new best friend, and went and paid for the textbooks I thought I could afford. Then I spent a week just getting through my crazy life. Whenever it got too bad, I went back into my mostly empty bedroom and looked at my Christian Friends flyer. That thing was getting raggedy around the edges by Wednesday night.

I was really surprised by the number of cars in the church parking lot when I got there. If you'd asked me how many people would attend a church meeting like the one I was going to, I would have said maybe half a dozen. This parking lot had a couple of dozen cars in it, easy. Surely they had to be here for something else. The place looked big enough to have several classrooms and such that people could meet in.

I had found Conejo Community Chapel on the first try, even in the dark. The map on the flyer was good. It helped that the building was recognizable as a church. It even looked like some of the churches in Cape Girardeau, Missouri, which was my gold standard for churches, although it wasn't like the one my Granny Lou had gone to there.

That one had been the most imposing, and maybe the most intimidating church I'd ever been in. This one was a nice homey little church built out of brick, with actual stained-glass windows.

The look of the church was typical of what surprised me at many turns in Southern California. So much of it was a slightly twisted version of Mayberry. Sort of like you took Mayberry and blended it with Hollywood, so that everything is slightly off-kilter.

On one hand you had seventy-five-year-old churches nestled in groves of trees, and then the new California intruded and you'd run into a guy in a Hawaiian shirt, black rubber thong sandals, jeans and a cell phone glued to his ear as he went into the building. Chances are good he was the kind of guy who was church council president and tithed, too. Like I said, Mayberry meets Hollywood. It was decidedly odd, but I liked the whole feel. In fact, it was beginning to grow on me. For everyday wear, I'd more or less adopted the jeans and black sandals thing myself. Hawaiian shirts, too, for that matter. When I was feeling a little unsure of myself, like tonight, I at least wore a tame one.

When I got into the building there were little handwritten signs on cardboard that made me feel vastly relieved because there were several other things going on. I could have gone to an AA meeting, it looked like, or some other kind of loud support group cheering for somebody who was meeting in one of the Sunday school rooms just down the hall from the kitchen.

Now that I was here I was a little nervous. It felt like the first day at a new school, where you don't know where your locker is and you haven't found the bathroom and you're sure you're not nearly as cool as the popular kids. Didn't like that feeling in junior high school and wasn't any fonder of it now, thank you.

It was moments like this that I understood why smokers smoked. At least they had something to entertain themselves with and something to do with their hands. Maybe if I had a cup of coffee, life would be better. I could smell some brewing someplace, but it didn't seem to be coming from the kitchen where the Christian Friends meeting had been listed. I headed that way, anyway.

There was a woman who looked like Linnette from the back, stacking up chocolate-chip cookies on a plate on the counter. Naturally, chocolate chip. My least favorite, but I'm the minority. Everybody else thinks they're wonderful. I was just glad to see somebody familiar. Her hair made me want to ask that stylist question while I still remembered it. Finding a good hairdresser was better than cookies any day. "Hi. Coffee ready yet?" I asked in what I hoped was a breezy, cheerful "I've been here forever" kind of voice.

"Nope. The can's in the refrigerator and the carafe for the coffeemaker is broken again, so if you're desperate you can wrestle Big Bertha." She didn't even turn around to look, so she couldn't see the face I made. So much for knowing all of the insider stuff.

"Uh. And Big Bertha would be…" My confusion got her turned around, and now she was the one making a face. "Oh, phoo. I'm sorry, I thought you were Dot. You sound like her a little and I guess I just wasn't paying attention."

"Nope. Still Gracie from the bookstore."

"Please, please, don't flee in terror because some wacko made you get your own coffee the first time you came to a meeting. Pastor George would shoot me."

She redeemed herself right there. Anybody who said "Oh, phoo" was my kind of woman. "Don't worry about it. I won't tell. And I'll even make the coffee if you'll tell me where the pot is."

She gave me a conspiratorial smile. "Welcome to Christian Friends. The coffeepot is Big Bertha, and she's huge and under that cabinet. You want to hold the pot, Gracie, or fill the water?"

"I'll hold and you fill. That way you can figure out how much coffee to make for whoever you expect. There were so many cars in the parking lot I didn't know what I was getting myself into." We wrestled the coffeepot into position near the sink, where thankfully there was one of those faucets on a flex line where Linnette started filling.

"It's not that intimidating. Probably six or less will show up. This is way too much pot for the coffee we need, but we need some, so there it is. Dot should be here any minute. Lexy will be late, because she saves all her timeliness for her work as a corporate lawyer. Once she goes off duty, she slows down. Heather will be even later, if she makes it at all. I'd go into Heather's problems, but we don't have that much time. Probably Paula will show up, as well, if nothing else more pressing comes up." Her nose wrinkled and I wanted to ask about Paula, but just then we got company.

A lady maybe seventy or so breezed in, and I marveled again how different California people of a certain age looked, compared to the Midwesterners I was used to. They dressed younger out here for one thing, and almost everybody was tan year-round. Unlike a lot of California ladies, though, this woman was letting her short, curly gray hair stay gray. It was silver, really, and looked very nice.

She wasn't rail thin, but definitely thin enough to make the capris and tunic-type T-shirt she wore look good. The mule-style sandals she wore had sensible, shorter heels and she had fire-engine-red polish on her nails, fingers and toes. "Dot—great, you made it," Linnette said, putting the lid on the coffeepot and plugging it in. "Dot Morgan, meet Gracie Lee…"

"Harris," I said, sticking out a hand to shake. She had a nice handshake. "It's so nice to meet you. And I really like that shirt." I was babbling, definitely.

If she thought I was babbling, Dot didn't show it. She had a real thoughtful kind of look on her face and I wondered what that was about. Maybe I had one of those familiar faces for her. "Nice to meet you. You're new here at Conejo Community—that, or you go to late service."

"New. I've never been to the church. Linnette found me in the campus bookstore a week ago." Now I knew I was babbling, but Dot was still gracious.

"Good," she said. "We can always use new blood." Between the coffee beginning to perk in the background and these two down-to-earth women, I felt right at home. This was going to be just what I needed.

"So what does Christian Friends do, actually?" I asked my companions a couple minutes later when there were four of us sitting around in chairs waiting for the coffee to be done and for a couple more people to show up.

The newest arrival was Lexy, who was one of those tall, slender blondes in black leggings. She would have made me nervous—or at least intimidated—if Linnette and Dot hadn't been there first. As it was there was just enough cellulite in the room to make me less conscious of my despised derriere.

"Drink coffee and talk, mostly," Linnette said. "Listen to each other's problems. Not to solve them exactly, but more to just listen." She didn't get any further in her explanation before three more women hit the room at once. They couldn't have been more different. One was tiny and Asian, close to fifty probably, and already talking when she got through the threshold. There were two conversations going on actually—one directed at the women who came in with her and one at somebody on the other end of a tiny cell phone.

"Paula," Linnette mouthed in my direction under the stir of the women coming in. The second one had to be Heather. She was a limp-haired pale blonde in her early thirties who might have been quite attractive under other circumstances. However, she had the circumstances of a damp pregnant lady, which doesn't tend to make anybody look attractive. Her black leggings were baggy at the knees and pouched a little at the seat, and her pink rubber sandals squished underfoot. The third woman had to be her mother. She had the same blond hair, a face that relayed what Heather would look like in thirty years if she didn't use a lot of sunscreen and wore a sour expression to rival Paula's.

Before I could say anything, Paula plopped herself down at one end of the semicircle of chairs and opened a portfolio. I don't dislike many people on sight, but in her case I could make an exception. Between the cell phone when she came in and her overall perfection, she looked like the type to drive me nuts. "All right. Why don't we get the meeting started? I'm sure some of us are in a hurry *to go home.*"

She glared at Heather and then gave me the fish eye. I could see what Linnette had meant in her few words earlier. If I hadn't decided to dislike her already, her words to Heather would have swayed me.

Paula was a pain in the neck. I could tell that much from my first five minutes of getting to know her. Anybody who actually cared that Heather was getting the floor wet, and said so, instead of worrying if she was going to catch pneumonia or something, had to be a pill. Everybody else in the group seemed to be real pleasant, so I guess Paula had to be the "one" there is in every crowd.

Linnette appeared to be in charge here, and she didn't seem to like Paula all that much, either. She masked it better than I probably did. "Paula, you know we don't take notes here. Christian Friends group stuff is confidential. That means what's said here stays here."

Paula sniffed. "I remember that. But I have to write down things about the phone call I just finished. It's about a very important closing tomorrow." I should have figured she was in real estate. "Besides, you have all the beginning stuff to go through. You won't get back to me for ages."

Linnette shrugged, sort of a "whatever" look on her face, and went through what appeared to be a set opening to the meeting. She explained a little bit more about Christian Friends, we had a brief prayer and she offered anybody who wanted the chance to get a cup of coffee. I took her up on it, and noticed that Heather and the older woman with her did, too.

"We have one newcomer tonight, and a few others who are still fairly new to the group, so if we could make introductions…" Linnette looked down the row at people, and I hoped that I wouldn't have to go first. It felt like junior high again in here.

"I can go first, because I'm not really here for myself anyway." The older blond woman spoke up. "I'm Sandy and I'm here because my daughter needs help."

Hoo boy. And I thought Paula was going to be the resident pain. Sandy, here, was definitely in the running.

As if that weren't bad enough, her daughter was nodding. "I know it sounds awful, but she's right. I do need help."

Linnette looked like she wanted to say something, but didn't get the chance. Heather went on. "Six months ago, my life was perfect. I had a job I loved, a nice apartment, had met the guy of my dreams, the whole bit. Jack was a little older than I am, but he was witty and charming and funny. When I talked to him, I felt like I was the only woman in the world."

I hated to hear the "was" portion of what Heather said. Didn't sound like this was a relationship with a future. And I felt all misty over her description of Jack. I'd had one of those guys myself, before he went and drove his car down an embankment.

"Anyways, all that fell apart when I went and got pregnant. I waited a couple weeks to be sure. Maybe if I'd told Jack right away when I thought I knew what was going on, things would have been different." She was trembling now, but I had news for her. She didn't just go and get pregnant. Ol' Jack had helped a whole bunch, and now I was not so thrilled with him, suspecting what came next.

Heather was twisting a handful of tissues now, and her voice was shaky, but she went on. "I finally told him and he just blew up. We had this screaming fight where we said things I'm pretty sure neither of us meant. Five months and four days ago, Jack Peterson walked out of my apartment and just vanished."

Her mother made a face like she'd swallowed lemons. "Of course you never called the police."

Heather shrugged. "Mom, he's a healthy grown-up. We weren't married and he didn't even live with me full-time or anything. Isn't it enough that he canceled his cell phone and there wasn't ever any new activity from him on our joint credit cards? I think that told me what I needed to know."

"Well, it didn't tell *me* anything. I want to find out how to hit that jerk with child support. Maybe even some kind of legal damages, with the kind of distress he's caused you. You lost your job—"

"It's a sabbatical, Mother." Heather sounded tired. This seemed to be a conversation they'd had before. "I just started it earlier than I'd planned."

"Well, there's precious little money coming in, either way." Sandy rolled her eyes. Maybe I'd be just as dismayed to have my adult child come home pregnant, unmarried and with her life spinning out of control this way. I hope I'd be compassionate instead. Maybe it was a good thing Heather was here, even if her mother dragged her. Everybody else looked a little more compassionate than her mother.

"We'll be okay." Heather sounded braver than I could have been. For that matter, she sounded braver than I felt in my own current situation. She was rummaging around in her bag. "You asked if I had any pictures last time," she said, looking at Linnette. "I finally managed to dig one up. It's not all that good, just a printout from my digital camera on photo paper. Jack wasn't much for having his picture taken."

She passed it to Linnette, who looked at it and smiled. "He's quite handsome."

"Show it to everybody. You might as well all see the guy I've been crying over." Heather motioned, sounding wistful.

Linnette passed the picture around, with everybody looking at it briefly and passing it on. Then it got to me, and after a glance I started to pass it on to Dot. But then I couldn't. I looked at it again, hard.

This couldn't be. Maybe I was seeing things. I reached for my own wallet and pulled out the one studio shot I had of Dennis. It didn't take much comparison for me to feel very, very ill.

I must have suddenly looked as awful as I felt, because even Heather was looking at me strangely. I passed my picture over to her along with her own. "I think I might have an idea of why there's been no activity on that credit card." I handed her the photo. "I'm Gracie Lee Harris, and I'm here because one night in August my husband, Dennis, drove his car over the side of an embankment and nearly died."

Heather looked down at the picture. "That's Jack." Her voice was small and panicky.

"No, that's Dennis. And he's been in a coma for five months. And he's definitely, without a doubt, already married to me." Wasn't he? Seeing all this gave me more than a few doubts. It also made me lose it about the same time Heather did. This looked like the end of anything else worthwhile happening at the Christian Friends tonight.

"I'll get more tissues," Linnette said.

"And maybe a bucket," Dot added. I looked over at Heather. As pale as she was, Dot's idea might have been a very good one.

2

"This can't be right. It can't be happening," Heather said, ending on a wail.

I wanted to agree with her, but I couldn't. It was happening, and the crazy thing was, it made sense in the oddest kind of way. Dennis having another woman on the side explained plenty of things.

Linnette and I were the only ones left in the room with Heather. Heather's mom had been the first to bail, followed quickly by Paula. I have no idea where either of them went, but nobody seemed to miss them much. Dot and Lexy had stayed for a while to try and help Linnette calm us down. Heather was too upset to say much. She mostly muttered or sobbed instead.

"You know, a lot of things in my married life look different when I take this into consideration," I said to the two of them. "How long have you known Dennis, um,

Jack?" It was hard to know what to call him around Heather.

"Almost two years. We really hit it off, but he said he'd…uh…just gone through a bad divorce…"

She trailed off and I could finish the sentence for her, "And then he said that maybe you would be the one to restore his faith in the female half of the human race. And could he move in while you got to know each other better—right?" Even his lines didn't change from woman to woman.

"Oh, no. You mean you heard it, too?" Heather wailed again. "I should have known something was funny. He was gone so much of the time on business."

"And he never gave straight answers about where he was. Or the money he was spending." She nodded in agreement. Something else dawned on me, and it made me even more ill than I'd been before. Had he even intended our marriage to continue once he moved to California himself? Knowing Mr. Charm, he was ready to break things off then, but just couldn't do it.

We were surrounded by most of a box of tissues littered around the floor and our laps, and Linnette patted my hand when I needed it. That was fairly often. I was in better shape than Heather, but not by a lot.

I still felt sick and dizzy, and every time I stopped to remind myself to breathe, a new question popped up. It seemed to be the same for Linnette, at least the question part, because she kept asking about things she could do. "Do you want me to call Pastor George?"

"No," Heather and I answered in unison. I don't know about *her* reasons, but I figured the time to meet the pas-

tor for the first time was not over this debacle. Not tonight, anyway.

"All right, then. We'll wait a while on that, shall we?"
Linnette nodded.

"Yeah. I think I want to go home." Heather gave me a
plaintive look. "Would you come by tomorrow and take
me to the place where Jack is? I have to see this for myself. I keep thinking that maybe this is a mistake. Maybe
it's not him after all...."

Why did I feel a hysterical laughing-and-crying fit coming on? Oh, I know. It was because my normally weird and
horrid life just got ten times worse in the space of one hour.
My head hurt, and I was real glad I'd never gotten around
to those cookies. As it was, the coffee wasn't exactly sitting well. There was a bitter burning at the back of my
throat that I hadn't experienced since I was pregnant with
Ben. I could only imagine how awful Heather felt.

I was pretty sure what she'd discover at Conejo Board
and Care. The man she called Jack Peterson was my husband. That wasn't going to keep me from taking her
there, though. No matter what it was going to do to my
life, this was a young woman who needed some closure,
and I could probably give it to her.

I took a deep breath. "Sure. What time should I pick
you up?" I had classes in the morning, but so what?
School might just go on the back burner for a while.

We settled time and directions and everything, and
then Heather looked around the room for the first time
in a while. "How am I going to get home?"

"Maybe your mom is still here someplace. Do you
want to go looking for her?" Linnette stood up, and we

both followed her. A quick check of the building didn't yield any sign of Sandy, so we headed for the parking lot.

There was a big Lincoln idling in the rain in a parking spot close to the church. "That's my mom. At least she waited for me." Heather sounded so plaintive I wanted to hug her.

She trudged to the car and got in. I was just glad to see her lovely, sympathetic mother hadn't locked her out. Linnette and I watched the Lincoln peel out and then looked at each other.

"Last time you'll invite a stranger to your group, huh?" I said. I expected her to agree with me, but she shrugged instead.

"Nope. I'll keep doing it. This whole mess was meant to be tonight, Gracie. God has reasons for things. Nothing that strange happens by coincidence."

Even in California, I felt like adding. She was right, though. Heather and I would never have met on our own. She might have gone through years of wondering what happened to her fiancé. I, meanwhile, would have been blissfully ignorant of what Dennis had been doing on all his business trips around the state, but surely there was something good that would come out of this knowledge, as well. I just couldn't figure out what it was right now.

"I think it's time we both went home," Linnette said softly. "You okay to drive?"

"I think so. There should be some interesting conversation with my mother-in-law once I get home. For a change I almost hope she went to bed early."

That, of course, would have been too easy. If I'd wanted to talk to Edna about things that couldn't wait, she would have gone to bed by the time I got home. There seemed to be days at a time when we only met at the care center in Dennis's room or over a rare, silent dinner.

Tonight she was still up, sitting at the dining room table reading the paper. I'd almost forgotten, before moving in with Edna, that you could get your news that way. Shows how computers have warped our lives.

"That's just out of the question," Edna said ten minutes later. "Becca is coming tomorrow and visiting her daddy. There just won't be room for another person in the schedule."

"Well, we'll have to make room. It's important for Heather to see him for herself." Of course it was important for Becca, Dennis's daughter, but she hadn't exactly been beating a path to his door so far. The few times she'd come, she'd timed her visits to avoid me. I suspected that was on purpose. We had yet to meet in the time that I'd lived in California. That was just the way Becca wanted it, apparently. Tomorrow was shaping up to be a dandy day.

"Couldn't she wait a day? It's not like it's really probable that this man she's looking for is Dennis," his mother argued.

"Oh, I think it's more than probable. I think it's about a ninety-five-percent certainty that the man she calls Jack Peterson is Dennis."

"Peterson? He called himself Jack Peterson? Oh. Well, maybe she ought to come along." Edna's color was pale suddenly and her voice was soft and hesitant. Something about that name changed her mind. That was a shame, because I was almost hoping she'd been right before. It would be a giant relief to me if Heather came tomorrow, looked at Dennis and said that she'd been mistaken. Now I was back to believing that wasn't going to happen.

"I think I'm going to bed. Looks like I'll need the rest," I told Edna. Not that I expected to sleep all that much.

Normally at night I got on the computer to trade instant messages with Ben for a while. Instant message sessions with one's own offspring no longer struck me as a weird or unusual event. Before the accident, instant messages had been one of my major forms of communication with Dennis, as well. He roamed the state with a laptop, and it was cheaper than the cell phone.

When I was instant messaging with Dennis it had been cool. With Ben, I probably found out more that way than I would have if he'd been in the same room. Typing on the computer he tended to forget once in a while that it was his dear old mother on the other screen. Of course I had to put up with some of the same language he would have given his chat-room buddies occasionally, but it was a fair trade-off for the breezy, open conversations with my son. Being that he was seventeen, that was worth gold, especially when we were separated by this many miles.

Tonight I was too tired to deal with Ben's high energy level. Besides, what would I tell him? "Oh, by the way, your stepfather is still in a coma, but now he seems to have a pregnant fiancée." That wasn't communication that would fit in an instant message, at least not for me.

I picked up Heather the next morning about eight. Heather looked better dry and fixed up. Her jeans and white oxford shirt looked pressed and neat, and her hair was combed.

The fun began at the Conejo Care Center ten minutes after we got there. We sat in the family lounge where there seemed to be unwritten rules about the seating arrangements. Edna would sit next to me or next to what I assumed was Becca, but the four of us couldn't sit together. Especially not after Heather showed up, which drove the other two across the room to talk in low whispers. We were all waiting to go into Dennis's room while they finished his morning cleanup and a little physical therapy.

"So much for being one big, happy family," Heather said. "They do know who I am, don't they?"

"Edna does. Becca, the daughter, hasn't even met *me* yet. So don't expect her to get real chummy. It will get better, though. We all have one very important thing in common." I tried to sound a lot more hopeful than I felt, watching those two in their corner.

This was all so surreal. I should hate Heather. In all probability she was carrying my husband's child. But somehow this vulnerable young woman was harder to hate—or at least dislike strongly—than Dennis's blood relatives, who had never been pleasant to me. None of them was worth a lot of distress anyway. I personally was going to save my fighting until Dennis was strong and well enough to be my adversary. If that ever happened.

Before the accident, I'd thought Dennis and his mother were one big mutual admiration society. But even their little permanent lovefest hadn't prepared me for Edna with her grandchild.

Becca had her father's chocolate-brown eyes, blond hair and a rounder face than I'd expected from Dennis's daughter. Before the accident he wasn't skinny, but there were definitely more angles to him than curves. Becca ran toward curves in a big way. Maybe her mother did, too. I hadn't ever met Carol, either.

Of course Edna insisted on going into Dennis's room with her first when the aide said we could head in. "Becca's got to go to work later. She won't get much time to see her daddy," Edna said as they breezed past me into his room. I wasn't about to argue with either one of them, so I stood there in the waiting room and hoped one of them would come out soon. Four were too many to put in that room, especially when they weren't getting along.

Twenty minutes passed and we were still cooling my heels. "This is crazy. Come on." Heather followed me and we went across the hall. If the nurses glared, I'd live with it. I caught Edna's eye hoping that she'd be genteel and introduce me to Becca. Instead she huffed and left the room.

Awkward, I decided, is meeting your stepdaughter for the first time over her father's prone body.

"Hi. I'm Gracie Lee. I'm glad to finally meet you."

She didn't offer a "me, too" or even a "likewise." Just eyed me up and down and went back to staring into her father's face.

"And this is Heather Taylor," I said, motioning next to me. Heather was as rapt looking at the prone form between us as Becca was.

"I know who she is. Nana told me while we were having breakfast." Becca didn't sound too thrilled about the knowledge. Of course, she'd been avoiding me all this time, so what could she possibly think of another interloper like Heather, this one even younger and prettier than her evil stepmother?

Heather reached out and stroked Dennis's hand. "Was I right?" I almost hoped I wasn't, but her expression had already told me that Dennis was Jack Peterson. The way Edna reacted last night to the name had given me confirmation that Dennis had led a double life. I made a mental note to ask her why that tipped her off.

"He may still be quiet, but he looks a lot better today." And he did, too. I wasn't just saying that. Maybe the staff's projections that he could be coming around were something we could start believing. I hadn't wanted to before, just not to be too hopeful. It had been months now, and we hadn't seen much to be hopeful about.

"I have to leave for a minute." Heather's lip was trembling. "I'll be back."

"Good riddance," Becca muttered under her breath, just loud enough for me to hear as Heather fled. I started to snap at her, but then held back. Dealing with this kind of trauma took you back a step. I could remember back five years to when my dad died. Even at thirty-three, I'd felt younger than my twelve-year-old son. I could just imagine what it would do to your mind when you were only in your early twenties, and Becca couldn't be any older than that.

"Hey, this is a shock for her. Imagine if you had told someone you were expecting his baby and he promptly disappeared."

Becca shrugged. "No such luck. I married Brandon first, and then had the baby. That's the way most people do it."

"I know, but Heather didn't get that chance. And now I imagine we're all short of sleep dealing with all of this." Becca made a face.

"Yeah, well, even if I wasn't coming here I would have been short of sleep. Ollie's teething and he kept me up most of the night."

"That's your son? How old is he?" It was strange making small talk like this, but what else could I do?

"Eight months. I bet you think that's a weird name— Ollie."

I wasn't going to agree with her, even though it did sound a bit odd. But then, "Abigail" is right back up on the hot names list for little girls, and it sounds like something from 1890 to me, too, so who was I to say what was odd? At least he wasn't named Hunter.

"His daddy is a skater. Semipro. So he's named for the trick."

Hmm. I had no idea what Becca was talking about. Not a clue. Sometime later today I knew that Ben would be rolling his eyes all the way from Missouri when I asked him about all this. So I'm a hopeless, clueless old person. Sue me.

We both shut up at that point and just paid attention to Dennis, each on our own side of his bed. After a couple minutes Becca broke the silence. "The nurse in here earlier said she thought he might be waking up. That he's had some eye flutters and stuff."

She sounded hopeful but a little withdrawn. If there had been evidence of the eye flutters while I'd been in the room, I'd missed it. He looked so much better, though, anything could be possible.

"I hope she's right." Not for the same reasons that his daughter did, probably. Mine were less unselfish by now, and I wanted a lot of answers to questions.

"Come on, Dennis. We're all pulling for you." I squeezed his hand and thought I felt a squeeze in return. Maybe today was the day everything got better, or at least clearer in this strange new life of mine.

Throughout the morning, visiting time was tense, to say the least. As it happened most days when I was there for longer periods, the staff would occasionally boot everybody out to deal with Dennis's needs of various kinds. When they let us back in at eleven I thought I was going to have to arm-wrestle Edna for first dibs in the room. I held my ground, though, and insisted that Heather was going in first and I went in with her. Nobody else was going to join her, that was for certain.

We stayed about fifteen minutes and switched places with the Peete women. By the time they came out of Dennis's room I was ready to lay down the law.

"This has got to get more civil. If they're right and Dennis is finally waking up we could be in here together for days. Once Dennis is really awake it will stress him out if he sees us fighting. Why don't we practice getting along now so that it's second nature by the time we need to?" It all sounded reasonable to me, but not to Becca.

Her lip curled and she stepped away from me. "Why don't we not? I don't see any reason to get along with either of you. Nana and I will go have lunch next door. Maybe when we get back you'll be gone or something."

"Wow. That was real mature." Heather watched the two of them retreat.

"My life feels like a high school soap opera right now. Nothing is mature." Standing up suddenly took too much effort, and I plopped down on one of the benches.

My husband's fiancée was actually consoling me while we waited to see if he'd come out of a coma. This was *worse* than a soap opera, I decided. When Becca and Edna came back from their lunch, Heather and I went out to eat. By now I was pretty familiar with all the offerings in every place in the strip mall next to Conejo Care.

We settled for the deli in the Ralph's supermarket. At least today it was nice enough to eat outside at the picnic tables in the center. Nothing looked real appealing, but I got the better looking of the two soups out of a kettle, and a roll to go with it. Maybe I'd actually drop some of the twenty pounds I always wanted to lose while life was crazy.

Maybe not, I thought as our route back took us past a high-end coffee shop. Heather got a dark roast decaf while I decided on healthier green tea for a change. Tea from one of these places was another one of those things that stumped me at first in California. Instead of a normal tea bag, every place did these custom designer things that involved loose tea in a long open bag that got tucked into the rims of a pair of cups put together. I figured it was to make it all look worth the two bucks or more a simple cup of tea cost in these places. I also got a cookie for myself and two cups of herbal tea for Edna and Becca. It couldn't hurt to come bearing a peace offering.

It was received coolly, to say the least. Edna took the tea with very little enthusiasm, said, "Thank you, Grace" and set it down beside her on a table.

Becca looked at hers as if there were a bug floating in it instead of a tea bag. "You didn't happen to ask what's in this herbal tea, did you? I'm still nursing Ollie and there's a lot of stuff out there I wouldn't want to pass on."

That might have been a little more information than I wanted. "Plain old Lemon Zinger." I couldn't recite the ingredients list off the top of my head, but I didn't think it involved anything you wouldn't want to share.

"Oh, well, thanks just the same, *Grace.*" I told myself I would not growl at this aggravating young woman, who was perceptive enough to sense the tension between her grandmother and me, and pick up what Edna called me. Other things demanded my attention right now.

We still had more than an hour until two o'clock when they would let us back into Dennis's room after lunchtime and therapy. If Becca really was leaving to go to work, she sure wasn't rushing any. So here we all sat in separate camps. I didn't see any of the other family groups acting this way. There seemed to be groups of two and three people together everywhere acting more civil than the four of us. But then, if two of those groups were really warring factions of the same family, how would I know?

"This is so strange." Heather was sniffling a little. "You'd think that we could all talk about Jack—I mean Dennis—together. Try and figure out what we're going to do in a day or two when things are closer to normal."

I hated to tell her, but normal was going to be a relative term from now on as far as I was concerned. "Did

Dennis mention being married after Carol?" It had been on my mind since I found out about her.

Heather blushed. "He said he'd had a close call. But he wanted to hold out until he was really sure about things, so he waited…." Her lip was trembling a little.

Great. So I was "a close call." How strong was Dennis's heart? I wondered if it could take waking up to the two of us sitting by his bedside together. If he woke up lucid, I'm sure he'd have an explanation to take care of everything. Looking back on our life together, Dennis had never lacked for glib explanations of a lot of things.

I reached over and took a sip of my tea. It wasn't piping hot anymore, but it was still drinkable for a little while. "This is really ridiculous, Heather. If you and I can call a truce, you'd think those two could join in. What have they got to lose?"

She stood up, wiping any lingering tears away from her face. "I'm going to go find out."

She did, too. Marched right across the room and sat down in an empty chair close to them and started talking. For a few moments it looked like they were going to ignore her, but even Edna didn't have that much willpower. Especially when Heather was asking about her favorite subject, her son.

"His middle name was Jack, you know. When he was little sometimes I called him Jackie. And my maiden name was Peterson. So maybe he wasn't stretching the truth so much after all."

The woman could put a good face on anything if it involved Dennis. As Granny Lou would have said, Edna was sure he hung the moon.

After a few minutes I sat down at the edge of the group, putting my tea down on the table next to Becca, where hers, I noticed, was still untouched. Amazingly, as if to make amends, she took a sip of it, and then grimaced. "Way too cold. How about yours?"

I nodded and she took both cups and went to the other end of the room where a doorway opened onto a kitchenette that family members were allowed to use. I could hear her put both cups in the small microwave to heat. She came back in a minute or two with our cups. I tried to pay attention to Edna.

She was still on Dennis's many accomplishments, having gotten all the way up to his speech at his eighth grade graduation. I think she knew that one by heart. And if I had to listen to that one again, I was going to go a little batty right here in this waiting room. But wasn't this what I wanted? Everybody getting along and playing nice?

Maybe this was just a little *too* nice. What was different about Heather that made the two of them warm up to her while treating me like something to be avoided? Now I was the one way too close to tears. Dashing past Heather, I finally obeyed my impulse to bolt out of this place. This place made me a little crawly on the best of days, and the oddities in this one had just gone past my endurance point.

The patio courtyard outside between Conejo Care and the strip mall was sunny again today. There was a gardener pulling dead blooms off some bright pink flowering plants around the base of a large tree. I still didn't know enough about California flowers to know what this one was called.

When someone came up behind me and laid a hand on my shoulder I just about levitated. I know I squeaked.

"Wow, what were you expecting?" Linnette Parks came around where I could see her. "I didn't think I was that scary, Gracie Lee."

"You're not. I was just off in another world."

"Does it include Heather? She called my place this morning and left a message about going to see Jack and where you all would be. I came up to see if the two of you were here, since I couldn't get anybody to answer the phone at her place and you hadn't shown up for school."

"She's inside with Dennis's mother and his daughter, Becca. I'm sure Edna is still regaling her with details of her son's charmed childhood and perfect youth."

There were those tears again. My hands were balled up in fists. Linnette, bless her heart, put her hands gently on my shoulders and eased me up off the bench. "Come on. We're going to take a walk or two around this parking lot. You need to blow off some steam and move for a while."

She was right. It took more than one round of the perimeter of the big double lot of the care center and strip mall before I could really put coherent thoughts together. Every time I got to developing a question out loud, another one cropped up even while I was talking.

"I mean, what do I tell Ben about this whole mess? And my mother? I can just imagine that conversation. She's never been that fond of Dennis from the outset."

Linnette just let me walk and wave my arms while she made sympathetic noises once in a while and walked along with me. It was amazing to me that she didn't jump right in and try to answer all these questions for me. Most people would have, even though there weren't any right answers.

Finally I ran out of questions, except for that one. "Okay, how come you're just letting me go on here without playing Dear Abby or something?"

We kept walking, at a slower pace now than the fast clip we'd taken off at. We'd been close to twice around the parking lot complex. "Christian Friends is basically a lay ministry program that helps people in crisis. And the first thing I learned in training is that God gave us two ears and one mouth for a reason. We need to listen at least twice as much as we talk."

We walked on for a minute more. "Thanks," I told her. "I don't need Dear Abby anyway. Maybe the name of a good divorce lawyer. We'll see in a couple weeks, I guess."

Linnette started to say something, but before she could get far, my cell phone started ringing in the pocket I'd shoved it in hours ago.

"This is Kara from Conejo Care. You need to get back up here immediately. Are you close to the center?"

"Almost at the front door," I told her.

"Then hurry. You won't believe what's going on."

I filled Linnette in and we started inside. Once we got out of the parking lot my nerves got the better of me and I stopped in the closest ladies' room. Kara was still bubbling ten minutes later when we got to Dennis's hallway. "Wait until you see what's happened. It's better than we'd ever hoped for. Come on and I'll fill you in as we go."

Better than anyone had hoped for? That was a switch. Kara was hustling down the hall and turning her head to talk so often I was afraid she was going to walk into a wall. Linnette was still trailing me. I'd insisted she come on along instead of waiting in the family room.

"About half an hour ago Mrs. Peete—Dennis's mother, I mean—came to the nurse's station to tell us that it seemed like he was coming around."

That made me glance at my watch. An hour had passed since I'd left the unit. With all the walking and venting with Linnette, I'd totally blown off the two o'clock visit. At least we were here now, and thanks to my stop, my hair was combed and I had lipstick on. If Dennis was going to see me for the first time in five months, I didn't want to look like a total wreck.

Kara was still talking over her shoulder. "I didn't think that was going to happen, but I went to see anyway. And he was moving and his eyes were fluttering open and closed. I told her she might be right and put one of the aides in the room to watch with her while I called the doctor."

"And then you called me."

We were at Dennis's room now, and she stood aside to let me go in first. There was no aide in there with him, and no doctor. Not even Edna, although her purse was still there, and paper tea cups on the bedside table with a teabag protruding from the rims.

Dennis was still there and sitting up in bed. But instead of the amazing changes we'd been promised, something else had happened. Even to me, with absolutely no medical training, it was pretty obvious that Dennis was dead.

The nurse's quick actions—also the blurted-out exclamation—confirmed what I'd thought to begin with, that Dennis was gone. She whisked us out of the room, and Linnette and I found ourselves sitting in the family lounge staring numbly at each other. I recognized from watching medical shows on TV that they "called a code" in Dennis's room, but it was over almost as soon as it began. First there were medical personnel racing down the hallway past us, and all too soon they were gathering in a knot outside the door to talk in hushed tones.

In a few minutes Kara came in to speak to us. "Mrs. Peete? I hate to have to tell you this, but…"

I wasn't even going to bother with reminding her that it was Ms. Harris. We'd been through this a dozen or more times and it just wasn't worth it right at the moment. "I think you already have," I told her. "Dennis was dead when we went in there, wasn't he?"

She nodded. "It looks like it. We'll have to call the police now. It's policy when there's an unexpected death," she said, pressing her thin lips together into a bloodless line. I felt like she was blaming us for this whole mess.

Linnette looked a little pained. "Do I need to stay for anything?"

"Just for a while. Once the county sends whoever they're going to send and they ask their questions, I'm sure you can go."

Kara looked like she was ready to leave, but I had a couple questions before she did. "Excuse me, but when I left here earlier, Dennis's mother was here. You wouldn't happen to know where she's gotten to, would you?"

There had to be a simple reason for her vanishing, like a trip to the bathroom or something, but even Edna didn't usually stay in there this long. And given the circumstances, I would have thought she'd be front and center.

Kara looked puzzled. "Let me go ask the nursing supervisor. I certainly don't remember exactly when I last saw Mrs. Peete. That is, the other Mrs. Peete…"

I figured it would be the last we saw of Kara for a while. By the time she explained the situation to the nursing supervisor, the woman would be so confused she wouldn't know *who* she'd seen all day. Especially when we added in the whole cast of characters that seemed to be missing, like Heather and Becca.

And while I still hoped there had to be a simple reason that Edna wasn't at the bedside when we got back,

I didn't hold out great hopes that she'd turn up soon. None of the rest of my life was simple; why should this be?

In an amazingly brief amount of time the medical personnel around Dennis's doorway gave way to people who obviously belonged to security, waiting for the police department. Now the fun was really going to begin. I tried to think about how we were going to explain everything to a police officer.

And where were Heather and Becca? What was going on here? Nothing made sense at all anymore. Somewhere in some of the recesses of my brain it was beginning to register that Dennis really was gone, but I was too tired and confused to cry yet. That would have to wait a while.

Heather wandered into the lounge looking dazed. "What's going on? While I was in Jack's room I started feeling sick. I still do that sometimes even when I'm not upset about anything."

"So you've been in the ladies' room? How long have you been in there, Heather?" Linnette's voice was gentle. It was so tempting to let her handle all of the difficult stuff that was going to come next.

"A long time. Why is Jack's door closed? And where are Becca and Edna?"

"We were hoping you were with them somewhere." I couldn't let Linnette do all the dirty work. "And as to why Dennis's door is shut, if you don't know already you better come sit down by us."

If she'd seen anything of what had transpired, Heather was a good actress. Her shock at what we had to tell her seemed very real. "But when I went to the bathroom, they had him propped up. He almost had his eyes open. His lips were moving."

Linnette looked at her watch. "It's about two-thirty now. Any idea how long ago this was?"

Heather shrugged. "Half an hour, maybe? I was pretty sick. There's a couch in the ladies' lounge, and I kinda lay down on it for a while, just to make sure I was really okay."

"Mrs. Peete?" A dark-haired man carrying what looked like a steno notebook stood by the doorway scanning the room. I stood up and he came over.

"Detective Ray Fernandez from Ventura County Sheriff's Department."

"Gracie Lee Harris." His handshake was firm. "Until yesterday, I thought I was Dennis's wife. Now apparently that's come into question. At least there's a question as to whether I was the only woman who thought she had claim on him, anyway."

"Yeah, well." He looked around. "Can we sit back down and let me ask you three some questions? I'll let you go first, Mrs. Peete."

"How about calling me Ms. Harris. Or Gracie Lee. I never did take Dennis's name formally, Detective. I have a son from my previous marriage and have kept that name far too long to change."

"Fine. So what can you tell me about what's going on here?" The detective tilted his head, alert and listening. Not a short black hair fell out of place. He looked like a Hollywood movie cop in plain clothes. The nubby charcoal suit jacket was a nice cut on his broad shoulders, and his white shirt almost sparkled underneath it. The jeans were either very old friends or stylishly worn. Without knowing him it was hard to tell.

"Very little. It appears that my husband is dead. I wasn't here when it happened, and it seemed to be a surprise to the nursing staff, as far as I can tell."

"You weren't here? Where were you?" His forehead creased. He also seemed to be looking at Linnette, wondering who she was.

"I was outside on the patio where I happened to run into my friend Linnette Parks." That answered both his questions at once and I hoped I'd get some brownie points for it.

"How did you know to come back up here, then?"

"One of the nurses called my cell phone and said Dennis seemed to be coming around. Either she was mistaken or waking up was more of a shock to his system than anybody expected," I told him.

Even as I said that out loud, a cold trickle of suspicion made me shiver. Why was I assuming that Dennis's death had been from natural causes? Apparently the staff hadn't thought so, because here was the detective. Nursing homes didn't normally call in the police when a critically ill patient dies, even unexpectedly. Did they?

"Have you been here alone most of the time in the waiting room?"

"No, and I'm wondering where the others got to," I told him. "Earlier this morning there were four of us. Dennis's mother, Edna Peete, was here and his daughter, Becca, from his first marriage, besides me and Heather."

"Your husband's fiancée." His voice was flat. He and Heather still hadn't said much to each other, besides introductions. Right now she was across the room, stretched out again, looking pale. I doubted she could hear our conversation from where she was, which might have been a good thing.

"Right." It still felt pretty strange to agree to that out loud.

"So, the other two. Where are they now?"

I shook my head. "I have no idea. When they paged me I came directly to Dennis's room, and there was no one else in it. Although I'm pretty sure that his mother is close by somewhere, because her purse was beside the bed."

"I'll go check on that." Detective Fernandez rose from his seat and closed his notebook. As almost an afterthought he looked around the room at the three of us again. "I'd appreciate you staying here until I got back."

It didn't take him long, and when he came back he looked puzzled. "You said Mrs. Peete's purse was by the bed. Could you come and show me where?"

I followed him into the unit, feeling uneasy now about going back to where Dennis's body still lay. I shouldn't have worried. Someone had taken pains to compose him, lowering the head of the bed and cleaning up whatever evidence of medical intervention had taken place. But there was no handbag by the bed. "Maybe it got kicked underneath while they were in here trying to revive him."

"I'll check to make sure it didn't get moved then." The detective looked like he didn't really believe it had been there to begin with. I was sure that Edna's large pastel bag had been next to the bed. Bending down I checked underneath the bed without going any closer to it. Nothing except a few bits of clear wrappers from something. Definitely nothing as large as a purse of any kind.

That was odd. I knew that Edna's bag had been here. Hopefully a member of the nursing staff picked it up to keep it safe. If not, what were the possibilities? Either somebody lifted it during the code or, almost as unrealistically, Edna somehow snuck back in here sometime in the past half hour and grabbed her purse. Neither made much sense.

Those were our choices, though, as I found out soon enough when the detective came back, a frowning Kara in tow. "There is no purse at the nurses' station. I know the one you're talking about, but I have no idea where it went."

"So you're telling me that some time in the past twenty minutes it just vanished?" I know I sounded sharp, but that was impossible.

Kara shrugged. "It sounds pretty lame once you say it that way. But I'll agree with you that it was here earlier. Probably. Mrs. Peete was in here, and you just don't see ladies of a certain age without their handbags." She was right on that score. Edna would have to be a patient in the care center herself before she'd be without that purse.

Ray Fernandez was frowning now along with Kara. "That doesn't leave us many options. Either somebody other than Mrs. Peete came in here and took that purse, or she was still here and took it herself. Are you sure you saw it?"

"Yes, I am. There were several things out of place, and that was one of them. The other was a disposable cup that looked a lot like the one I left in the waiting room. And it's still here." I pointed to the nightstand where the doubled paper cup still stood, the end of the teabag snagged between the two cups. It was the way most coffee shops made a cup of hot tea these days with their fancy designer teabags. The cardboard jacket around it was gone, but it was otherwise intact.

"Was he drinking liquids like that?" The detective sounded decidedly suspicious.

Kara shook her head. "Not yet. If he was really coming to the way we thought, that would have been the next step. But it would have been water first, and monitored by the nursing staff. Somebody besides staff had to help him to that."

Great. If I was right, it was my tea, in my cup, with my prints all over it. And somebody had probably fed it to Dennis, illegally, sometime in the half hour before he died. I was thankful Linnette and I had been in a very public place in front of lots of witnesses. At least I wasn't going to be the one blamed for breaking all the center rules.

The detective was using his cell phone. "I don't want anything else touched here, including Mr. Peete," he said to Kara, then whoever was on the other end of the phone answered. "Yeah, this is Ray. I need two techs and the van at Conejo Care Center. Second-floor critical care wing."

He ended his call and looked at the two of us. "This is officially a crime scene until we know differently. For the sake of the other patients in the unit we'll forego the yellow tape, but otherwise we'll be playing by my rules from now on."

A crime scene? I figured Dennis's death might be suspicious, but not a crime. A horrible, unexpected accident, or maybe even a bit of negligence somehow. But the look on the detective's face told me that he considered it a lot more serious than a mistake on the part of the center.

He was looking at Kara now. "Is there a private room nearby we can use for Ms. Harris? And I suppose we'll need to put your friends in there, as well," he said, turning his attention toward me.

My friends. *Friend* was a funny thing to call Heather, but there wasn't much of an official title for whatever she was. Linnette might not claim being my friend if this mess got too much more complicated. I'd only known her for a couple days and here I was, involving her in the worst mess of my life without ever meaning to. So much for the start of a beautiful friendship. I'd be lucky if she'd speak to me after today.

Kara's solution to the room problem was to commandeer the family waiting room, posting a sign on the door and closing it off. It was large enough to put all three of us in separate corners where we couldn't talk to one another. There was also the attached kitchenette. I suspected it was normally where doctors met with family members to hold consultations that weren't going to go well. As such, it was the perfect place for this detective to take each one of us alone while the other two sat and stewed. Linnette and I sat in our corners while the detective spoke with Heather. Fortunately Linnette was a lot more gracious about waiting with me than she could have been.

She made a quick, muffled call on her cell phone, smiling weakly when she was done. "Well, that's a first. I had to tell my supervisor that somebody needed to cover for me because I was forbidden to leave by the police. You should have heard his reaction."

"I'll bet. If I've gotten you in trouble at work, I'm so sorry. When the detective comes back in I'll try to see if he can't let you go."

Linnette waved a turquoise beringed hand at me. "No, don't worry about it. This is interesting in a weird sort of way. And I'm not leaving you here alone to deal with all this. Besides, the cop's kind of cute. Did you notice a wedding ring?"

I hadn't, but it wasn't exactly high on my list of things to pay attention to. "No, and given my situation, we can say it wouldn't necessarily make any difference. Now hush. I think he's coming back."

He was, and still wore the unhappy expression he'd had earlier. "Nobody answers at your mother-in-law's home. Ms. Miller's husband tells me she should be at work right now, but doesn't have the number."

"Ms. Miller? Oh, I guess that's Becca." It was difficult, answering your own questions. I guess I had to, though, because Ray Fernandez didn't look like he was likely to answer mine any time soon. "And it's just vaguely possible that Becca could have gone to work before all this heated up. She'd been saying most of the morning that she couldn't stay much longer because she had to get there."

Ray shook his head. "Ms. Taylor says they were both definitely in the room the last time she left. Not that anybody can verify her story, either."

I had another thought. "Do you have Carol's number? Dennis's first wife?" At least I *thought* she was the first Mrs. Peete. She had to be. Becca looked older than twenty, and even Dennis probably wouldn't have married straight out of high school, would he? I couldn't say anymore.

"No. Do you?"

Maybe this would earn me a point or two with the growling detective. "Yes, and she would have her daughter's work phone, as well, I imagine." I dug around in my purse for all the odd little slips of paper I'd scrawled things on, including phone numbers. "She might even have heard something from Edna. It wouldn't surprise me if they kept in fairly close touch."

I'd bet that if Edna had called anybody, wherever she was, it was more likely to be Carol than anyone else I could think of at present. There was just something about the way Edna spoke about the mother of her grandchild that told me *she* was still Dennis's wife, as far as his mother was concerned.

"While we're at it, can my friend speak to you and go back to work? I don't want to inconvenience her when she was kind enough to check on me in the first place."

Linnette waved me off again. "Hey, no good deed goes unpunished."

That got a smile, granted a wry one, from the detective. "You're right, there. If you want, Ms...."

"Parks," Linnette supplied. She tilted her head in a charming manner, and following the angle of her subtle gesture, I could see that the detective wore no wedding ring, for what it was worth. "And I cleared it with my boss at the College Bookstore, if you need me to stay. He'd probably be happier if I went back to work, but I don't want to hinder your investigation."

"Nice to have somebody say that," he grumbled. The man was really beginning to get under my skin. That was a shame, because it looked like I was going to be seeing more of him than I was anybody I liked better for the next few hours. Or maybe even days. At this point even Edna's company sounded better, and it would have gotten me off the hook besides.

Of course, that in itself was a reason that I probably wasn't going to see Edna for quite some time. She'd never accommodated me yet, and I didn't expect she'd start now.

Linnette went into the kitchenette with Officer Friendly and Heather and I kept to our separate corners as instructed. I don't know what we might have said to each other if we'd been allowed to talk. Looking around the room there was no evidence that the four of us, or anyone else for that matter, had spent part of the morning here. Either someone from the staff had been in and cleaned, or a patient's family member had tidied up after everyone.

I suspected it was the staff, and could more than likely guess the person who cleaned up, although I didn't know her name. Most afternoons and evenings that I'd been at the care center the same Latino woman, slight, neat and mostly silent, came through the entire wing. She mopped every floor and emptied the untold tons of trash that accumulated in the place. It made me feel bad at this point that I'd seen her for this many months and still didn't know her name.

With her on duty, staff cleanup was more likely, unless some patient on the hall had been "sinking fast" as

Granny Lou would have said. During those times, a lot of the family members dealt with their antsy spells by tidying up the lounge. Right after Christmas, when one dear old soul had a series of small strokes over the course of a week, her daughter and daughter-in-law had done everything in here but crochet doilies for the vinyl couches.

Still, it would be hard to show any proof to this detective that Edna and Becca had been with us all morning. I hoped that Kara and the rest of the nursing staff had seen them coming in and out.

It still bothered me that Edna's purse was gone. There hadn't been any reports of stuff going missing the entire time Dennis had been here, so I had to discount theft. That meant that Edna, and maybe even Becca, had been here when Linnette and I had come up. Where had they been, and how had anyone gotten back in the room to get that purse?

I was still working that over in my mind when Linnette and Detective Fernandez came out of the kitchenette, looking chummy as old friends. "I'll let you get on back to work now, Ms. Parks. I've got all your phone numbers and until we know differently, you're a material witness, so don't leave town." He seemed to be perfectly serious and Linnette nodded and shook hands with him.

She stood in the room halfway between Heather and my corner. "You heard the man. I'm heading out of here. But either of you, call me if you need anything. Okay?" We both nodded, and she left.

"So what happens next?" Okay, being blunt might not endear me to this police officer. At this point I figured nothing I did was going to endear me to him. Heather certainly wasn't in any shape to ask questions and somebody had to.

"Next we stay right here until the evidence techs finish up across the hall, and the ME—that would be the medical examiner—has come and gone. I watch all of that going on in between talking to you two, and we decide who's going to go back to the station with me."

I hadn't considered that part. Did this mean that this was really a homicide, and Heather and I were suspects? It was a scary prospect and getting more likely every minute.

"Are you going to try and find Becca and Edna?" I certainly wasn't going through all this alone when they'd spent the morning with us, not if I had to.

"I'll do what I can without leaving here. But none of the three of us are leaving this building until after Mr. Peete has been transported to the morgue. After that we'll be leaving together."

Heather was heading toward the exit again. She had a look on her face that was getting familiar by now. "She's not trying to flee," I told the surprised detective. "She's had stomach problems every hour or two since I met her last night. Some pregnant women do. If you want me to follow her, I will. Or we both can."

He headed toward the door himself. "Let's do that. I don't really want to let her out of sight long at this point."

He was going to have to let her out of sight for a few minutes, given where she was headed. I got the feeling that Detective Ray Fernandez had a challenging day in front of him dealing with Heather. He didn't look like the type used to sick pregnant ladies. Given his general demeanor so far, I couldn't feel very sorry for him.

The door to the ladies' room was still in motion when we got to it. There were signs from the other side that Heather was obviously in there doing exactly what I'd predicted. The detective stopped me at the doorway. "This is as far as either of us is going."

"But what if she needs help?"

He looked grim. "We'll call a nurse. They're probably used to things like that."

Not for that cause, but I suspected he was right. I started to open my mouth and protest that I was plenty able to help Heather take care of herself, but then it dawned on me. This guy wasn't going to let us alone together in case we were in cahoots on whatever had led to Dennis's death. I still thought it was likely that they'd discover that this was all a terrible mistake. *I* knew I didn't kill Dennis, and it was hard to imagine that any of the others had, either.

Apparently it was easier for the detective to imagine, because we stood guard over Heather's doorway for a solid ten minutes and then all went silently back to the family lounge once she appeared. There were several people carrying equipment and cameras going into Dennis's room across the hall when we got back. This was going to be a very long afternoon and I was already tired of it.

The Ventura County Sheriff's Department shares a facility with the Rancho Conejo municipal police. It is every bit as glamorous as you'd expect a suburban sheriff's station to be: a big, squat tan-brick-and-concrete structure with a lot of steel and limited glass. I'd driven past the building quite a few times, but never noticed much about it before.

Now, with the prospect of seeing a lot of it from the inside, it looked even less appealing than it ever had while I was driving by. I reasoned that things couldn't be too bad because at least Detective Fernandez had let me drive over here myself. When he discovered that Heather and I only had one car between us, he'd balked at us driving over to the station together, though. At least she sat in the front seat of his unmarked car with him on the trip. And I'd noticed following them over that he didn't have to make any stops for her to throw up, so perhaps she was less upset than she had been before.

I was still pretty upset. This day had gone from bad to worse already and didn't show any signs of turning around. When I pulled into the visitors' lot at the sheriff's station, I wondered how long my poor car would sit there before I could go home again.

The detective and Heather were waiting for me on the pavement outside the building. Pulling into the parking lot reminded me of something I'd wanted to point out to Detective Fernandez, and I hurried over to the two of them to do just that. "Her car wasn't in the lot when we left. Edna's car, I mean."

"Right. An older blue sedan. I could tell you the license plate number if I looked at my notes. And you're right—it wasn't there, although one of the nurses who came into the building at the same time as Mrs. Peete and her granddaughter this morning did say she thought she saw them getting out of that car."

Okay, so maybe he wasn't as set on me or Heather as the only possible suspects as I thought. If we really were suspects. I kept hoping that somebody would turn around and say, "Oh, our mistake. Dennis wasn't murdered after all. Everybody can go home now." Maybe everybody was just being ultracautious so that we didn't sue the care center for neglect, or even the hospital that had transferred him there months ago. If that were the case, though, where were Edna and Becca? There were probably a dozen good reasons why they weren't here, but I couldn't come up with any of them at the moment.

The detective ushered us through the front doors of the station and we went down a broad flight of stairs. It was a busy place, with folks that looked like sheriff's deputies, other employees and regular old civilians coming and going. We went through another set of double doors downstairs, then into a waiting room. "Detective Division," Fernandez said, motioning to the spare environment. "This is where you'll come back to once we take your prints. I'll take you over to processing now so that we can do that."

It was an inky, messy process, but the woman doing the work was efficient, and she had a canister of some kind of wipes that took most of the ink off pretty quickly. Then she made one phone call and then Fernandez was back to usher us across the building again.

Detective Division still looked just as stark. "I have to take your statements and make a few calls. Then we'll decide what to do next. If I can get you something to drink while you wait..."

"Nothing with caffeine in it," Heather said. She did look frazzled enough already. "If you have any kind of lemon-lime soda, I'd take that."

"Same here." Maybe if I acted more agreeable for a while the detective would stop scowling at me. He got us settled in uncomfortable plastic chairs in the waiting room. They reminded me of the ones at Pacific Oaks, strewn through the hallways next to professors' doorways where students waited for appointments. There was no way to settle into them comfortably.

In a moment the detective was back bearing two green cans. "I want to make two or three calls, then I'll talk to you both. Get as comfortable as you can. It won't take long."

I wondered if Ray Fernandez had ever sat in these chairs. If he had, he'd know that any time in them felt like too long. Next to the doorway into what I assumed were the detectives' offices there was a desk with a phone and computer where a young woman sat entering something on the screen. "This is Jeannie. If you need anything, tell her. That includes if you need to leave the room for any reason." I felt like I was in junior high detention but I kept that information to myself. Still trying to be agreeable, or at least seem that way.

Ray Fernandez's idea of a short time turned out to be twenty minutes or more. It was long enough for Heather to finish her soda, need to go to the bathroom and manage to still be gone (with the lovely Jeannie in tow) when the detective came back. His consternation was obvious when he came into the room to find me there alone. Had he expected Jeannie to take me to the bathroom along with Heather, or to call someone else to watch me?

"Detective, Ms. Taylor is over eight months pregnant. She's tired and nervous and you gave her a full can of soda to drink. Figure it out."

He looked confused for a split second, and then I would have sworn he almost blushed. "Ah. She and Jeannie are down the hall? Then why don't you come back with me and make a statement?"

I followed him into another room with as much charm as the rest of the sheriff's station. This one might have been even less attractive than anywhere but the room where we got our fingerprints taken. It was a large room split into a warren of cubicles, eight or nine at least.

A couple of the cubes were occupied with men or women, mostly on the phone or computer. More were empty. In Fernandez's cubicle, the furniture consisted of a desk, a computer and phone much like Jeannie's, one comfortable office chair and two more of those horrors from the front room. Of course the comfy chair was behind the desk.

The plastic ones here weren't any more comfortable than the ones outside. I hoped I didn't squirm too much and look uncooperative or even guilty somehow. "So, what's the word on finding Edna?"

Fernandez sighed. "I'll ask the questions, Ms. Harris. You provide the answers. But just once I'll answer one of yours. We haven't found Mrs. Peete yet. Would you know if she has an answering machine at home?"

"She doesn't. I've suggested more than once that we get one, but she won't get caller ID or an answering machine. Which means we talk to every telemarketer in three counties."

He gave me a questioning look. "We? As in you live with your mother-in-law?"

"I do. Dennis moved out here to start a business, and to save money he moved in with her. Once our home in Missouri was sold, I moved out, as well. Before we could do anything about looking for a place, Dennis had the accident that put him in Conejo Board and Care."

His forehead creased. "I'm familiar with that. I was the detective who did the reports on that case, as well. He was driving *your* car, wasn't he?"

This was more than I wanted to remember. "He was. We'd switched that morning because he said his was making a funny noise and he wanted his favorite mechanic to look at it. He took mine and by evening it was totaled and he was in the hospital."

"During the time after the accident until today, was he ever able to speak to you about what happened?"

I wasn't sure what this had to do with today. And if he had done the initial reports, surely he knew. "Detective, if you took the earlier notes, you know what happened. Dennis hasn't been fully conscious since the accident."

He tapped a pen on the desktop in a brisk rhythm. "I'm sorry, Ms. Harris, but I do have to ask questions. And if you had been more cooperative in the past few months I'd have answers to some of them already."

"More cooperative? I have no idea what you're talking about."

"Nobody ever answered the phone at your home, there was no e-mail address anywhere for you and the postcards I sent requesting that you call never got any answer, either."

This felt like a battle brewing. "As I told you before, there's no answering machine in the home I share with Edna, so that's why you were out of luck on that score. I don't remember talking to anyone afterward to have left an e-mail address with and I have never seen any postcards."

"Fine. Suit yourself." I was surprised at how effectively somebody with such soft brown eyes could glare.

"I will. But trust me, there hasn't been a lot of communication between Edna and me in the past four months.

She's not much of a talker. For that matter, I hadn't even met Dennis's daughter, Becca, until today."

"Not what you'd call a close family, is it?" He almost sounded sympathetic.

"To say the least. The only thing we all have in common is Dennis." I started to get teary once I'd said that. It was dawning on me that I should have said Dennis was what we *had* in common. None of this seemed real yet, even when I looked down at the traces of fingerprint ink still left on my fingertips.

He seemed to sense my discomfort. "Well, we need to get going here. No sense in leaving Ms. Taylor out there any longer than necessary."

He looked at his notes. "I think you've told me your legal name is Gracie Lee Harris. Is that right?"

"It is. I am—was—legally married to Dennis Peete, but I didn't take his name."

"Just for the record, has it ever been anything else, or do you go by any other names?"

How detailed did he want to be? I didn't want to be accused of not cooperating again. "Well, the name on my birth certificate was Robin Anne Mitchell. That's what my mother stuck me with, and my father let her.

"He called me Gracie, as in Grace Allen, and I added the Lee part. It always fit me better than Robin Anne. When I was seventeen I worked the entire summer and into the fall at Edward R. Spence Plastics trimming the rough edges off toy telephones. I made enough money to go down to the St. Louis County courthouse the day I turned eighteen and change my name legally to Gracie Lee Mitchell.

"The Harris part came two years later when I married Hal. I kept it after we divorced fifteen years ago, and this is all probably more information than you wanted."

Detective Fernandez looked a little dazed. Then he cracked the edge of the first grin I'd seen. It made him look years younger. "Yeah, maybe. But it beats too little information, and I should have figured that since I'd just told you that you weren't cooperating, you'd fill me in. Now maybe in a few less words you could explain how you and Ms. Taylor happened to arrive at the Board and Care together this morning, and what happened after that."

Surprisingly, it did take less time to tell him all of that. There was a little bit of detail to go into on Christian Friends and what they were and how I'd found out about the group at Community Chapel. After that he'd already gotten most of the information one way or another and I was just verifying my parts in everything.

"So, when you left to cool off, as you put it, Ms. Taylor, your mother-in-law and Ms. Miller were all still in the family waiting room?"

"That's right. After lunch Dennis had physical therapy and a clean-up, both of which they preferred to do with all of us out of the room."

"Was it usual for there to be that many people together in the family lounge?"

"Not for us. Normally it was only me or Edna. Sometimes we'd overlap. And once in a while on days I haven't been there, she's mentioned that Becca came to visit, too. But this was a rarity."

"And Ms. Parks, your friend from the group you mentioned. Did she come into the building at any time?"

I started to shake my head, and then corrected myself. "Not before I met her outside. But she did come in with me when I got the phone call during our walk. After that she stayed until you got there and talked with her."

"Do you know anyone else that would have cause to wish your husband harm?"

"Not really. I don't think from what he said that his first wife, Carol, was all that fond of him, but I can't see her doing anything violent. But then I've never met her, either. I could be wrong."

"What about business associates?"

"If I could track them down, I'd be able to tell you more. So far that's been one of the biggest frustrations after Dennis's accident. He left precious few business records where anybody could find them, and his PDA never turned up after the accident."

Fernandez gave me a strange look. "That's because we kept it as evidence. Didn't anybody tell you that? Somebody had to have signed for it after the crash, verifying that we kept it."

I shook my head. "Never. I'd like to see that record if you could dig it up."

"Definitely."

"Why did you keep it, anyway? In a routine accident like that, I can't imagine what good it would have done you."

That comment earned me another strange look. "Routine accident? That's hardly what I'd call it. Your husband was forced off the road. You can't tell me that in all this time, this is the first you've heard about it."

"I can and I will." Suddenly I didn't feel very well. This was just more information than I needed on top of everything else today. Panicky energy made me stand up, and my facial expressions must have conveyed my feelings.

"The ladies' room is right next to where you had your prints done. I'll send Jeannie after you. Don't wait for her."

Finally, some compassion from this detective. That was a good thing, because I needed it now. I couldn't have waited for Jeannie or anybody else without causing a lot more ruckus than I'd already been part of today.

Fifteen minutes later I was still shaky, teary and I wanted my mom. But I was out of the bathroom and back into the hallway with Jeannie. "Don't worry about coming back too soon," she told me, handing me another lemon-lime soda. "Ray brought the other lady in to talk to, and told me to make sure you didn't leave, but to be nice to you. He must feel bad about something. That's the only time he says that."

"And it can't be very often, from what I've seen already," I grumbled.

Jeannie raised an eyebrow. "You've got to be kidding. Ray's a teddy bear compared to most of the detectives. And he's probably the best closer in the county."

"Closer? I only know that as a real estate term, and I have a feeling that isn't what you mean." We were strolling back down the hall to the Detective Division.

Once we got there, Jeannie motioned to the padded side chair next to her desk. "You look like you could use a more comfortable chair. Those plastic things are awful. I meant 'closer' as in 'case closer.'"

"So he gets results?" She nodded. I sank down into her chair. Jeannie was right. This was a lot better on my back than the plastic things. But then again, a rock would have been better than those other chairs.

I just wanted to sit and sip my cold drink and recover some shreds of sanity for a while. Jeannie appeared to have enough work at her desk to let me do just that. When her phone rang I nearly jumped out of my skin.

"Good afternoon. Ventura County Sheriff's Department, Detective Division." She listened a moment. "He's in his office. Who can I tell him is calling? All right, just a moment." She gave me a speculative look, then shrugged and punched a couple buttons on her phone. "Ray? One of the women you asked me to put through is on the phone. Yeah, that's right. Okay."

Hanging up, she had almost a guilty look. I wasn't sure if it was for hiding information from me, or for saying as much as she had with me sitting there. Given that she worked for the sheriff's department, it had to be for what she might be giving away. Still, I decided to try my luck. "Please tell me that is my mother-in-law, Edna Peete."

She shook her head. "Sorry. I'm not allowed to give out information like that to anybody but the detectives. Ray would skin me if I actually told you who it was on the phone. Although I don't imagine he could do much if I told you who it wasn't."

"Which means it wasn't Edna. Which is just nuts. I can't imagine where she went. The woman is seventy-six years old and will be beside herself when she finds out about Dennis."

Unless she already knew. It was an idea I hadn't considered before, somehow. With everything else that had happened today, I hadn't stopped to think about Edna being truly involved in whatever had happened in that room. But then, if Heather hadn't done anything to Dennis, and the only other two women who'd been there were gone, they probably left together.

So if the person on the other end of that phone talking to Fernandez wasn't Edna, it could be Becca. It could also have been a lab tech, maybe. I glanced over at Jeannie's phone console in time to see the solid light blink out. On the systems I was familiar with from my previous jobs in a Missouri grade school and a junior college, that meant the call was terminated.

It was more difficult now to sit and try to relax and sip a cool drink. My mind was racing again with all kinds of possibilities. And Heather was still in there with Fernandez.

In a few moments she was out, still looking pretty shaken, but at least she was upright. She was pale, but didn't show any signs of needing to throw up again, so maybe she was getting a little better. If this had been a horrible day for me, I couldn't imagine how much worse it had been for Heather.

Ray Fernandez didn't look that great himself by now. He came out of the inner office rubbing his temples like a man with the beginnings of a nasty migraine. The tightness around his eyes looked like another symptom of the same thing. Maybe I'd been too hasty before when I thought he was glaring at me.

"I'll save you asking any more questions. That call was your stepdaughter, Ms. Miller. She claims to have left the care center about one-thirty this afternoon in the company of her grandmother. According to her they drove to the restaurant where they'd both had breakfast, she picked up her own car from that parking lot and went to work. She says she has no idea where her grandmother went from there. Ms. Miller claims she just now arrived at her mother's house where my message to phone in was waiting."

"Now you know that's already wrong, because Edna and her purse were still around the care center an hour after that. And Heather saw them both after two anyway." I looked at her for confirmation.

"I sure thought it was after that. I could have been wrong, I guess."

I wanted to scream. Didn't this woman have any backbone at all? My biggest worry right now was that she was going to accommodate herself into a stay in the lockup, and possibly take me along for company. I couldn't imagine how anybody could hold either of us for anything right now, but after the rest of today's events, anything could happen.

"I'm aware of what you've already told me, and what Ms. Taylor has said, as well. And before long there should be some initial reports from the crime lab to tell us more about what happened, from their point of view. In the meantime, Ms. Miller is going to come back here and give us some fingerprints."

Something about her timetable finally struck me. "Did you have to tell her about Dennis? Because if she really had left when she said she did, she would have no idea…"

"That he was dead? The thought had occurred to me, too, Ms. Harris. As had the idea that if she was right about the way things happened, her grandmother would surely have gone straight back to the care center. I checked there again just to make sure that she hadn't made an appearance." His expression was firm enough that he didn't need to verbalize the answer. Edna was still on the loose somewhere.

"So, can we go now?" Perhaps that wasn't being as co-operative as possible, but I was so incredibly tired.

"I don't know. I'm going to need more information from both of you. It would be easier to get if I requested that you stay here for a while longer, and you agreed."

The way he phrased that told me that there wasn't any way for him to hold us legally. I decided to press my luck just one more time.

"Look, Detective Fernandez, I promise I am not going anywhere besides home. And unlike my mother-in-law, I will answer any telephone call made to me, hopefully in three rings or less. I'll even bring Edna in here to get her fingerprints taken and make a statement, should she show up there. But this has been a long, horrible day and I'm getting very tired of public institutions."

His smile didn't quite reach his eyes. "You and me both. I don't know why I should trust you, but I'm going to. Don't leave town. Don't even leave that house unless you have a very good reason. And count on me calling no later than tomorrow morning."

"It's a deal. Thank you so very much." I hoped that sounded as grateful as I felt. Maybe Jeannie was right after all. Maybe behind the wolverine exterior I'd seen before, Ray Fernandez *was* hiding some teddy bear qualities.

Edna's house was empty when I got there. It was hard to think of it as home anymore. It hadn't ever felt much like home, and now that I knew that Dennis was never coming back to it, this house would never feel like home to me.

It was almost seven in the evening, which meant that it was almost nine in Missouri. At least I knew that my mother would be home, unless she'd talked Ben into taking her somewhere. She hated driving at night, so that was one of their arrangements. She packed his lunch and did most of the laundry; he did the night driving. I didn't really want to know what other deals the two of them had made.

When the phone was on its fourth ring I almost hung up. Then just as my mom's voice on the answering machine kicked in, so did her normal voice, sounding a little rushed and breathless. "Just a minute. Don't hang up." The recording stopped and Mom was back again. "All right. Hello."

"Mom?"

"Gracie, honey? What's the matter?"

The tears came fast and furious now, and I slid down to sit on the floor in Edna's kitchen. It was just too far away to walk over to the kitchen chairs. "Wrong? Everything. It's awful, and an unbelievably long story."

"Are you okay? I must sound funny because Ben's looking at me wanting to know what's going on. We were just walking in the door from getting ice cream."

That made me almost smile. I backhanded tears off my face and got up on my knees to snag a paper towel for my damp cheeks and runny nose. "I'm okay. Physically at least." I could hear her sigh, then reassure Ben. "It's Dennis."

"Now you told me yourself that you didn't think he was going to come around." There was true sorrow in her voice and I knew why I'd gone straight for the phone to call my mother. Even though she had never liked Dennis, she felt bad for him and for me and for all of us. "Do you want me to tell Ben, or do you want to do it yourself?"

"I'll tell him what I know, after I talk to you." There was an honest-to-goodness wail building up from deep in my chest, and I fought to push it back. Even as bad as things were, I didn't want to scare my mom over the phone. "But I don't know that much yet. And the stupid part is, Dennis actually was starting to come around, and then he died. Mom, the police think maybe somebody killed him."

"Ben went in the other room. Maybe you shouldn't tell him that part." It made me shake my head. My mom was protecting her grandson, even though he was now taller than she was by at least a foot.

"I won't right away." And I wasn't about to tell either of them that I'd seen the inside of a police station. "As soon as I know more I'll call you back and give you details. Now I guess you ought to let me talk to Ben."

"I will. But you take care of yourself, will you? Is Edna there? At least you can look out for each other."

I didn't want to get into all of that yet, even with my mom. Maybe I was protecting her as much as she wanted to protect Ben. "She's still out taking care of some business. But she'll be back." At least I hoped so.

"Good. And I'll tell Ben that when he's done not to hang up, that I want to talk to you again."

Now I knew Mom was rattled. Normally she was so conscious of long-distance spending, even on somebody else's nickel, she didn't want to waste a word. It was the first time all day anybody had been overly concerned about me. I was going to need the whole roll of paper towels before this conversation was through.

5

The next morning I sat nursing coffee and dreading to hear the phone ring. I figured the detective would be calling once he got into the office and got his act together, and I had no idea what to tell him. I felt pretty clueless about a lot of stuff right now. I should be planning what I needed to do, both for myself and in preparation for whenever they released Dennis's body to the family. There was a pad of scratch paper in front of me where I was trying to get organized enough to make a list. Any semblance of organization was slow in coming.

I'd slept little the night before, waking up to worry or listen to strange noises probably a dozen times. None of the strange noises were Edna coming home, which was also the biggest of my worries. I couldn't imagine where she was, or why she was gone for this long a time. She and I hadn't ever gotten along all that well, but I was still worried for her. It just wasn't like her to stay away from home this long for any reason.

Nothing was appearing on my notepad. Maybe I could start with a list of names of people I needed to get in touch with today. Edna topped the list, but I had no idea where she was, so even writing down her name was useless. Carol would be good, as would Becca. I had a few questions for both of them. It would be good to talk to Heather, assuming that she'd left the sheriff's department after I did. I felt a pang of guilt for not hanging around to make sure they released her, too. It wasn't a huge pang of guilt, because I couldn't have done anything to help her at that point, and I wasn't helping myself by staying anywhere near Ray Fernandez last night.

The person I really wanted to talk to the most was Linnette. She'd been such a sympathetic soul so far and I needed more sympathy. I also needed somebody with a clearer head than I had right now, and more detachment from all this. Before all the ruckus broke out at the Christian Friends meeting, Linnette had mentioned a roster list that she handed out to group members after their first meeting. Of course things got so confused that the roster never materialized. That was a shame, because it sure would have helped to have it now.

I needed something besides coffee and the echoes of an empty house. What sounded best was a doughnut…or three. On the chance that Edna would show up the moment I left to get some, I knew that I didn't dare bring a bakery box back into the house. She was a real health fiend when it came to sweets; it wasn't just cookies she kept a watch on. Anything with white sugar involved was

Edna Peete's nemesis. A bakery run sounded better and better, though. In a few minutes, the thought of sprinkles and chocolate energized me enough to put on my tennies, leave a note for Edna and put in a call to the sheriff's department. It was too early for Detective Fernandez to be in, thank goodness, but I left a message that I'd be available on my cell phone and headed out the door with it.

One of the odd things about California, at least for me, is the fact that while you can get a wheat grass smoothie on almost every corner, the smoothie store is probably next door to a doughnut shop. And a Starbucks, for that matter. But that's not just California. For someplace that is otherwise so concerned with youth, fitness and looks, there are an inordinate number of places to get junk food in Southern California. Those pink bakery boxes are everywhere.

Of course that's another shock to my Midwestern sensibilities. Who decided that bakery boxes were pink? Back in the Old Country a thousand miles in all directions from oceans, bakery boxes are plain white. The first time I saw a pink one out here, I thought it was a marketing gimmick. Then I discovered a second bakery and found out that out here, virtually anything Edna bears a grudge against comes in a pink box.

A brief three-block walk from the house was the closest cluster of pink boxes. There was also a market where one could acquire wheat grass, tofu and lots of grain and bean products in large bins. A nail salon, a few other shops and a restaurant or two rounded out the offerings in the plaza.

I stayed on the unhealthy side of the strip mall and got myself a sedate white bag with a few goodies in it. With only one of me to buy for, I couldn't justify an entire pink box. I got a cup of coffee, a glazed doughnut and a maple bar (which any sane Midwesterner would call a long john, but it's a maple bar out here).

It was too sunny to sit inside anymore. Just outside the doughnut shop was a large flat patio with benches on the edges all around, flanking the parking lot. The close-up view wasn't too scenic, but the mountains in the distance made up for it.

I sat with my coffee and ate one of the doughnuts. Even though this wasn't all that different from what I'd been doing at the house, it felt so much better. Here I was surrounded by people and activity and sunshine. All that almost felt good enough to abandon the sugar rush from the remaining doughnut.

A van pulled up in the parking lot and an older couple got out. With a shock of recognition I saw the woman was one of the Christian Friends ladies from Wednesday night, Dot. She and the man were wrestling a couple of big dogs out of the back of the van, clipping leashes to harnesses. A shepherd mix and something darker, maybe in the Lab family, hopped down to the pavement.

I tried to decide whether to say anything or not, given the way I'd torn up the meeting, but Dot made the decision for me by noticing me and calling my name as she went by. She walked over to my table and stopped and her dog, the Lab, happily plopped itself down at her feet, looking for all the world like it smiled hello.

"Hi. Buck, wait a minute," she called to the man and dog cruising on toward their destination. I had stood up by then and she hugged me, leash and all. "Are you okay? Linnette called me yesterday. I thought about you and Heather all night. What a mess!"

"You can say that again." I was beginning to be glad that a lot of Californians were huggers. It made up for my reluctant family. I told her why I was there and she gave me another hug for good measure.

The man and second dog were back by us now, and I could see that the old adage about people looking like their animals fit in this case. Dot's companion was a burly guy who might have looked stern if he wanted, but his blue eyes looked soft instead. He had a full head of sleek dark brown hair going silver and a mustache that was more silver with a few streaks of dark brown. All in all, he had the same coloration as the shepherd on the other end of the leash. "Honey, this is Gracie Lee, from our meeting the other night. The one I told you about."

"Ah. Hello. Buck Morgan." He held out the hand that wasn't holding a leash and shook my hand. "And this is Hondo." The dog's ears perked up at the mention of his name and his bushy tail beat time on the pavement.

"Glad to meet both of you." He had a nice handshake, and Hondo, once I held out a hand for him to sniff and had been accepted, had a great head to pat.

"Don't love on Hondo too much unless you want eighty pounds of dog leaning on you. He's a sucker for affection," Dot warned. "Seriously, though, are you all right? If I'd had your number I would have called."

Oh, no, here were tears again. "Honestly, I'm fine. Or as fine as I'm going to be today. But it's so kind of you to ask. I've just got a lot of sorting out to do. More now with Dennis's…accident." I couldn't say the "d" word yet, and wasn't about to let anybody else know it might be murder.

"Well, if you need any help, call me. Do you have a roster or even a church directory yet?"

"Not yet. I could sure use one." It would have Linnette's number in it, and Heather's—the one I needed most.

Dot gave her husband a look and he handed her Hondo's leash and was heading across the parking lot before she could open her mouth. "Buck's the head of the evangelism committee at the chapel. We always have a few extra directories in the van."

"So what are you doing here with a couple of dogs?"

"The vet's on the other end of the row. We have to keep their shots up extra good, and have their nails clipped regularly. We do volunteer work with them, but it's fun. Buck is probably one of the top dog trainers in the county, and these two are trained to be therapy dogs. We go up to the children's ward at the hospital on Thursdays, and the Alzheimer's wing at Conejo Board and Care on Tuesdays."

This was something that sounded good. Maybe when life got a little less crazy I could ask Dot how such things were done. Before I could open my mouth, we had a minor commotion. "Dixie, no! I hope you were done with breakfast." Dot was hauling back on the other leash as the remains of my maple bar disappeared into the belly of the smiling dog. I was pretty much done with the doughnuts, anyway, and Dixie looked like a very happy camper as she settled back down with a sigh.

Buck came back with a sheaf of papers with a golden-rod cover, stapled into a booklet, and handed it to me.

"Thanks, I appreciate it."

Dot looked at me sharply again. "And you'll call if you need anything?"

"I'll call," I promised, and meant it. We said our good-byes over protesting dogs and they got on their way to the vet's. I went back and got another two doughnuts to take home. Dixie had made them look pretty good.

It was still going to be the most wretched of days, but at least now I had Heather's number, and Linnette's. And my cell phone hadn't rung once. There was something to be said for all that, even on a day like this one.

It was still morning when Detective Fernandez called back, but it was a whole lot later than I expected. I'd gone back to the house and scrubbed the kitchen before the phone rang. There were actually a couple of notes on my list of things to do today and tomorrow. Maybe the amount of sugar and caffeine I'd put away wasn't a bad thing after all. Not to be repeated daily, but for today it worked.

The detective was actually pleasant on the phone today, a characteristic I hadn't associated with Ray Fernandez up until now. "I really appreciate you leaving me a second number. And answering it so promptly."

"I promised that if you let me go last night, I'd be easy to get hold of. I'm still home alone, though. Edna hasn't shown up here. How about there?"

"Not to my knowledge. No phone messages from her, either. Ms. Miller did come in and leave her fingerprints, though. Of course she managed to come in so early this morning that I didn't get to speak with her." He sounded aggravated about that. I could have told him that Becca was kind of aggravating, but decided to keep that to myself. I'd only met her once, under lousy circumstances. Maybe under the right conditions she was a delightful person. Given her heritage, I doubted it.

"What about Ms. Taylor?"

There was a silence on the phone for a minute. "Oh. She went home last night about an hour after you did. I think we had one of the uniformed officers drive her home." Bet that made a great impression on Sandy. If she thought her daughter needed help before, getting driven home in a black-and-white was only going to make things worse.

"Am I allowed to be in the same room with Ms. Taylor now and actually speak?" It was probably pressing my luck, but at least he was a few miles away.

"I guess so. Can I ask why you'd want to be in the same room?"

"Seeing as how she's my husband's fiancée, you mean?" It was hard to put my explanation into words, especially words a man might understand. I tried for the practical tack. "I'm hoping she has answers to some of my questions. Such as where the thirty thousand dollars I poured into Dennis's business might have gone."

There was a short bark of laughter or dismay on his end of the phone. "Yeah, well, good luck. I have a feeling Ms. Taylor may have the same kinds of questions for you."

I had that sinking feeling in the pit of my stomach again. It was getting more and more common these days. "Hey, maybe together we can come up with something. In the meantime, do you need me back at the station this morning?" I prayed silently that he didn't. The sheriff's department was the last place I wanted to be, even lower on my list than this empty house.

"Not right now. By Monday we will need both of you in here again. I'm hoping the lab will have all its answers by then, and perhaps we'll even get things squared away with Mrs. Peete. Why don't you plan on coming in about nine Monday morning unless you hear differently from me, all right?" He was taking charge of the conversation and being all official again.

"All right, Detective. I'll see you then." I hung up, hoping that his optimism on the lab work, and Edna's reappearance, would be justified. I didn't have any idea on the lab work, but I wouldn't want to bet with him on Edna showing up today. With every hour of daylight that she was still away, it felt less likely that she was coming back here anytime soon.

I looked around the kitchen, trying to figure out what I did next. I didn't really feel like sticking around in the house. It echoed weirdly with just me in it. There were still hours before I could talk to Ben either by telephone or computer. He'd taken the news of Dennis's death harder than I'd expected him to, but insisted he was going to school today anyway. I almost envied him the ability to do so. There was no way I could focus on something like school right now. This semester wasn't starting off too well for me.

I wondered if it was too late to drop my classes and recoup most of my tuition. Or should I go through with things, assuming that everything might get more normal soon and I'd want the distraction of classes to keep me

thinking about the fact that I was a very broke widow?
I certainly had more questions than answers.

At least I had an idea of what to do with the rest of my
day. I wrote another note for Edna and grabbed a jacket.
Somebody at Pacific Oaks would probably have answers
for my questions, whether it was a paid counselor or Linnette. It certainly sounded better than sitting here staring at the empty kitchen.

In an hour I was settled in at what I was beginning to
think of as "our" table at the Coffee Corner, sipping a vir-
tuously fat-free decaffeinated latte. Linnette was on break
to listen to me, and to add to the confusion, Heather was
there, as well. She'd apparently come in search of the same
kind of help I was looking for, going straight to Linnette
instead of making a fruitless stop at the counseling office.

"So tell me about it," Linnette said, stirring her coffee.
She'd gone with regular high-test, adding a little half-and-
half and sugar for sustenance.

"She looked twelve." Everybody in the counseling office had. I felt like adding "present company excepted"
on my diatribe on how young and inexperienced the
helping staff at the college looked. I knew Heather was
on sabbatical from a college job herself, and she didn't
look much older than the kids in the counseling office,
even though I knew from what she'd said that she was
over thirty. "It was confusing her that I was dealing with
the death of a spouse. Most of the people she talks to are
apparently upset because their grandparent has died, or
maybe a parent."

I guess that was why I'd always felt so comfortable in

the office at the community college when I'd worked there. The mothering instincts I'd picked up over the years worked just as well on the students and most of the staff as they did with Ben at home. It was rough being on the other side of the desk and being a student, especially a non-traditional one.

"I think it's because this is a four-year college, and private." It was Heather who was chiming in sympathetically, much to my surprise. "At the community college like the one where I'm on sabbatical, they're used to a wider range of students. Here the vast majority of the students are undergrads straight out of high school, still on Mommy and Daddy's money."

"It sure seems like it." The counselor, who had been all of twenty-five if I was being generous in my assumptions, just had no idea how to answer me. I silently thanked God and my grandmother's wisdom for leading me to the right place at the right time. I looked around the table, thinking that if Detective Fernandez could see this little coffee klatch he'd probably gag. Fortunately he wasn't here to see it.

Linnette looked thoughtful. "If you're going to drop your class, you basically have to do it today. Next week you'll get a lot less back, and the week after it's almost useless. Personally I might say stick in there. The profs are usually pretty understanding about major stuff like this, and you could always take an incomplete if you needed to."

Heather nodded. "I know I'd cut you a break if you were in one of my classes."

"What do you teach?"

She wrinkled her nose. "Comparative religion mostly. I'm the low woman on the totem pole, so I get the freshman breadth classes where there's two hundred kids in a lecture hall."

I felt sympathy for her. "And they're all rolling their eyes and raising their hands every twenty minutes asking 'Is this going to be on the final?'"

"Yes!" She was so emphatic she almost knocked over her hot chocolate. "How did you know that?"

"I worked at the community college in Missouri for years." And couldn't begin to say how much I missed that mundane, calm life right now. Tears sprang up again just thinking about it. It seemed like far too long since my life had been either calm or mundane. Of course, then I'd wanted more excitement. That was part of why I fell so hard and so fast for Dennis. Now excitement was the furthest thing from my mind; just coping sounded great.

"I think we ought to get the Christian Friends together more often than usual for a while," Linnette said. "Half the group didn't get to say anything this last time, and those of you that did get to say something need to say a lot more. I'll make some calls and see what I can do. That all right with you?"

I couldn't speak for Heather, but didn't have any qualms myself. "I'll be there with bells on, no matter when you set up the meeting."

Heather was nodding. "Me, too. But from now on I'm not bringing my mom. She means well, but I can only take so much of her sniping."

Linnette grinned. "I know as a mother, I should be horrified, but my first response woman-to-woman is 'good for you.' Don't you dare tell your mom I said that, though. I have to work with her on committees at church and she'll make my life miserable."

"Better you than me," Heather grumbled. For the first time in days I felt like laughing about something. Now why did that make me anticipate my cell phone ringing any moment with more bad news?

Half an hour later Linnette had gone back to work, but Heather and I were still sitting and talking to each other. I wanted to blame the nausea I felt on all the coffee I was drinking, but I couldn't.

"So how much money are you out?" she asked bluntly once Linnette left the table. "I figure if I'm as far in the hole as I am and I was only Jack's fiancée, you must be out a bundle."

My heart sank. I had been hoping against hope that my missing money would show up with Heather somehow. At least she was the person I would have begrudged the least, with no fiancé and a baby on the way. "Thirty thousand. I've been looking for bank accounts but so far no luck. How about you?"

"Wow, I was right. You have me beat by a long shot. I'm only down six grand so far, once I paid off the charges and stuff. Four of that went to the business, supposedly. Of course I've never been able to find the business."

"That makes two of us. The briefcase that I got back after the accident was full of invoices and computer-generated forms, but when I went looking for the address on the letterhead, it didn't exist."

"For me it was even worse." Heather slumped toward

the tabletop. "All I had was a phone number on business cards, and I knew it was Jack's cell phone. And that, of course, promptly stopped working once he disappeared. And then there was the Web site I'd set up for him myself, so I knew what good that was."

"There was a Web site for the franchise?" This was getting interesting. Maybe I could track something down from this after all.

Heather looked confused. "Franchise? No, this was for his own company. The pet weight loss by hypnosis thing."

There was hysterical laughter building in my chest again. Not only did my husband have two names, he had made two totally different lives to go with them. And he'd taken us both in so beautifully. I wanted to throw my coffee cup across the room, but I held back. There was no way to pay for the damage if the university sued me.

"Pet weight loss by hypnosis. Guess that isn't any worse than the franchise I thought he was going into."

Heather's face fell. "You mean we didn't even have the same business we were putting money into? Oh, great. What kind of franchise are we talking about?"

"Non-UV tanning beds with built-in aromatherapy. It was supposed to be the next big thing."

Now Heather looked like she wanted to give her mug a toss with me. "I think I can tell you what the next big thing was. It was us, or at least our money. And we fell for it, all the way to the bank."

6

I don't know what Heather did all weekend, but it was very quiet for me. The biggest thing in my weekend was finally making it to church at the Conejo Community Chapel on Sunday morning. I managed to avoid the service most of my Christian Friends buddies went to, it seemed, but it was still a nice place to be. And at the coffee and goodies time held after the early service I attended, they even had lots of things that weren't chocolate-chip cookies.

Edna didn't ever surface and I wondered how long it would be before I should think about filing a missing-person report. I'd finally broken down and told my mother the truth when I talked to her again on Sunday night, even though it meant dealing with her concern that I was there all alone.

The admission that Edna had been missing since Thursday afternoon when Dennis died got me plenty of concern. It even earned me a phone call back, not just from my mother but from my son. "You need somebody out there with you, Mom," he said, sounding so adult that tears sprang to my eyes.

I assured him that I was fine, and reminded him that I'd been on my own plenty of times in Missouri when he'd been at his dad's for long summer visits or camping trips with scouts. Still, he pressed me. "I want the number of that detective out there you told Grandma about, so that I can call if I'm worried about you."

I started to tell him that he should worry more about the detective getting me into trouble than anybody else, but stopped myself. Just because Ben was sounding like an adult didn't mean that he was one. I got Ray Fernandez's card and read the numbers on it off to Ben while he copied them. "I'm putting this right by the phone and the computer," he said, sounding more confident now.

It turned out to be a good idea that even calmed my mother down. I knew she had no desire whatsoever to come to California, especially since it meant getting on a plane, so she was happy to hear I was being looked out for. I assured her that I was, and we hung up again.

Once I was there alone again, I started thinking about whether I should call Ray Fernandez myself, and start the process of filing a missing-person report on Edna. Could I even do that? She was healthy, sane as far as I knew and in no one else's care. I wasn't a blood relative of any kind, so maybe I couldn't even file a report.

On Monday morning Heather and I marched into Ray Fernandez's office, positive we'd cracked the case for him. It didn't take long for him to disillusion both of us.

Seems he knew all about most of Dennis's shady financial dealings, and they even had a name.

"What we have here, ladies, is a small but efficient Ponzi scheme," he said, sounding more like a college professor than Heather did. He even had his hands steepled on the desk like a lecturer. "Does that phrase ring any bells with either of you?"

He had a wry smile when both of us shook our heads. "I didn't think it would. Forgive me for speaking ill of the dead, but your deceased husband and fiancé has shown most of the marks of an accomplished con man. And con men usually look for the same kind of victim over and over. For some guys, vulnerable women who can be charmed out of their life savings are the perfect mark."

I couldn't very well argue with him. In this case he was right. Dennis had always been perfectly charming; it was the nicest thing I could say about him. At least it was the nicest thing I could repeat in public. He'd always been so convincing about the piles of money he was going to make with his business deals.

Fernandez went on explaining Dennis's schemes to us. "A Ponzi scheme is like a pyramid. There have been a few big ones that have gone around the country any number of times in the past few decades. One of the biggest ones right now is something called 'gifting circles' that all too often involve women in dire situations." The detective's eyes darkened as he spoke, and I wondered if somebody close to him had been part of one of these 'gifting circles,' as he put it. "Mr. Peete doesn't seem to have ever operated on anything like that kind of scale.

He just married women, or nearly married them, and took their money one or two at a time."

"So where did it go?" Heather looked like she was ready to pound the table. "If this was a pyramid, there had to be a top to it. If that was Jack, or Dennis, where's our money?"

He sighed. "Your guess is as good as mine. He poured a little bit into those phony businesses he enticed the two of you to contribute to. He apparently paid off a part of his daughter's student loans. And once we find his mother, I'm ready to get a warrant to look at her bank accounts because I'm pretty sure we'll find some of it there. But I don't think all that will account for thirty-six thousand dollars."

Zowie. That sounded like a solid amount of money when you lumped it together. It was more than I'd made a lot of years back in Missouri when that amount supported Ben and me quite nicely. "So we're back to square one." I felt like crying, more out of frustration than grief at this point.

"Maybe not all the way back to the beginning. This verifies what I was afraid of—that there are a few people with enough motives to murder Dennis Peete." The detective looked at the two of us in turn, passing on the message that he apparently thought we were in that category.

I wasn't about to let that go unchallenged. "That's just silly, including us in people with a motive. Neither of us has any idea where our money's gone. And with Dennis dead, we're not likely to find out anytime in the near future."

Fernandez shrugged broad shoulders. "That's assuming that neither of you has found the money and concealed that fact from the other one, and now concealed it from me. It's also assuming that there aren't any more women running around thinking they're married or engaged to this man. Although I think we would have found them by now if they existed."

"I'm not so sure about that. If the two of us hadn't shown up at the same Christian Friends meeting, I still wouldn't know that Dennis didn't just walk out on me." Heather's eyes filled with tears. "Although maybe it would have been better just to think that. I think this way is more painful."

The detective spent some time looking down at his paperwork, scribbling something in the margins. It was almost as if he didn't know what to say to Heather. "I take it you haven't heard anything from Edna Peete?" he finally asked, turning to me.

"I told you I'd bring her directly here if I did." It was hard trying not to sound aggravated with this man. Maybe just the job he was in made him expect the worst of everybody. His tone of voice always sounded like he expected the worst of *me,* and I was tired of it. "No phone calls, no car in the driveway, nothing. How about Carol? Has she heard anything from Edna?"

"Not to my knowledge, and I've talked to her several times."

"Sounds to me like we're back to square one." Heather looked as dejected as she sounded. "And you're still sure it's murder, that the shock of trying to come out of a coma didn't kill Dennis?" I had to notice that she was calling Dennis by the same name as the rest of us did. It didn't feel like a good sign. Whatever hope she'd held in the man who fathered her child, it was gone now.

"I'm sure it's murder." It continued to surprise me that the detective's eyes could go from soft brown to glittering marble-hard so quickly. "In fact I'm surer than ever, now that the toxicology reports are in. According to the medical examiner this is officially a homicide, or at least manslaughter."

"How does he figure that?" The question was out of my mouth before I could stop it. I didn't expect the detective to answer me, but maybe for once I'd get a reply.

Wonder of wonders, he answered. "It seems Mr. Peete had a bit of GHB in his system."

Heather looked puzzled. "Like the date-rape drug, or the stuff that kids take at raves?" Fernandez nodded. "That doesn't make any sense. Could it be something that metabolized from something he was being given there by the doctors?"

"No. I already checked with the staff there, and nothing he was being prescribed bore even the slightest chemical resemblance to a date-rape drug. There's no medical use for the stuff for somebody coming out of a coma. In fact, there's no certified medical use for it in this country at all."

"So this would mean that nobody on the staff gave him this drug thinking it was medication. Someone would have had to have known they were giving him a street drug. Which is why you're calling this a homicide, right?"

His eyes were bright this time without glaring at me. It was a pleasant change. "Right. The amount he had in his system would only have made a healthy person mildly ill in most cases. It was the combination of the drug and his medical condition that killed him."

Fernandez was looking at me now in a more speculative way, and I felt cold and a little shaky. I had a feeling I knew what was coming next. "Did you find the drug anywhere else besides Dennis's bloodstream?"

"Just that cup of green tea that was on his bedside. The GHB there was in about the same concentration. I believe you said it was your tea, didn't you, Ms. Harris?"

"It was. But I certainly didn't bring it in there. I left that cup in the family lounge when I went out. And it didn't taste odd the last time I had any of it, either." Of course, none of this protesting was going to cut any ice with a police detective. I could probably have saved my breath.

"I didn't suggest that." His voice was calm. In fact it was almost too calm, making him sound like a snake charmer to me. I felt even colder than before, remembering what Jeannie out in the front office had told me about Fernandez's closure rate. "It would be helpful, however, if you stop by the department where you got your fingerprints taken before you leave the building. One of the techs there will take a DNA sample. It's a painless procedure, just a swab on the inside of your cheek."

This didn't sound good. "You also, Ms. Taylor. And I have one more request for you, although it's totally voluntary at this point. Is your obstetrician in the area?"

Heather's response was slow and puzzled. "She is now. I finally changed to one here in Rancho Conejo. I've spent so much time with my mother that it didn't make any sense to keep going where I'd started out, when it was a forty-five-minute drive. Why do you ask?"

"Because I think it might be helpful if you went and had a blood test yourself. I know you've told me that you've been nauseated most of your pregnancy, but that nausea you displayed the day Mr. Peete died was pretty spectacular. If there was GHB in one of those cups, it could have been in several, depending on how it got there. Not being a scientist or a doctor myself, I have no idea what kind of problems GHB might cause you or your child."

There were tears in her eyes now, and she was nodding. "I see what you mean. And it could have been something like that Thursday that was making me ill, or it could have just been the stress of a horrible day. But I'll call the doctor's office and see if I can get in."

"You might try to have that blood work done today. GHB doesn't stay in your system forever, and the longer we wait, the less we'll know for sure."

"Maybe I should just go on over there now." Heather's voice sounded shaky. I felt really bad for her, but then I'd felt that way most of the time I'd known her.

"Do you want me to take you? It might be better than going home to get your car and it would certainly be quicker," I offered.

The tears that had threatened before overflowed. "Would you do that? If I go home, my mom will see how upset I am, and it will only lead to bigger problems. Every thing I have to tell her about Dennis just makes her nastier to get along with."

The detective looked like he was about to say something, then apparently changed his mind. "We'll go get our cheeks swabbed first," I promised him. "Otherwise, are we free to go?"

He looked a little stunned. "Certainly. But do stop at the lab first. And when you get to your doctor's office, Ms. Taylor, please sign a release that will let them give me the information, as well, if you could."

"I will," she said, getting up from the chair with a little difficulty. While watching her gather her things and get ready to leave, I thought of the other thing I'd meant to tell Fernandez.

"You probably already know this," I started, and was thankful that at least he didn't roll his eyes. "But I thought of somebody who might be able to tell you more than anybody else about what actually went on in Dennis's room that day. Or any other day, for that matter."

"And that would be?" His notebook was out, with pen poised.

"I don't know her name, which is a mark against me, I think, seeing as long as I've run into her there. But the same woman cleans and disinfects everything in the family lounge and the patients' rooms on that floor of the care center every day. The only day I haven't seen her is Sundays."

Fernandez nodded. "I have a name here on my list of people to interview, someone from housekeeping. Adela Rodriguez."

"That might be her. This lady is somewhere in her fifties or sixties, I'd say, very slight build, long dark hair going gray. She always has a smile for everybody, but is very quiet except for humming. It always sounds like hymns to me." Which was funny, because they weren't hymns I knew. How I knew it was church music, I couldn't say, which is why I'd kept that part to myself instead of making a fool of myself again in front of Ray Fernandez. That had already happened enough times.

"Part of her silence might be because Ms. Rodriguez speaks little English, according to the notes I have here. That won't be a problem for me, but it might keep her from speaking to people there on the floor."

"True. Especially when she's dealing with people like me, who don't seem to have a clue even in English most of the time."

Fernandez stood up, shaking his head. "I wouldn't go that far, Ms. Harris. You're observant and seem to have a fair amount of feelings for most of the human race. Now go take your…friend to the lab and then get her to the doctor." I'd almost forgotten about Heather standing next to me. So much for not looking like a fool again. At least I didn't trip over the chair on my way out. It was the best I could say for my exit from the detective's office.

Heather's doctor was as reassuring as she could be, but that wasn't a whole bunch. She let Heather listen to the baby's heartbeat, which sounded normal as far as the doctor could tell. The blood tests she did wouldn't yield results for at least four days. Heather didn't look much more comforted when she came back to the waiting room. "She didn't find anything strange right away, so that's good." I didn't know what to tell her.

The past few days had been so terribly odd. I hated to keep bothering Linnette with all this, but there weren't too many other people who would listen to me or to Heather, either, for that matter. "Did you get Linnette's message?" Heather asked, almost making me jump. It was one thing to be thinking about somebody; it was another thing altogether to have the person next to you mention them at the same time.

"Not yet. Should I have?"

"Probably. She must have called you after she called me, and I got the message just as I was leaving this morning. I totally forgot to tell you until now. She called the rest of the group and can get Christian Friends together tonight on this short notice. Seven-thirty like usual." Heather had a wan smile. "I could use a good session of talking to other women."

"You and me both," I told her. I almost hoped nobody else had a crisis to deal with. There was going to be plenty to go around just with what Heather and I had to share with the group again.

Something else dawned on me as we were walking out in the parking lot to get to the car. "Are you up for one more trip this morning or not?"

Heather looked like she wanted to say no on the spot. "That depends on what it is," she said, sounding wary.

"Not fun stuff, that's for sure." I punched the button that unlocked her car door along with my own and we got into the warm car. "I need to make a visit to Dodd and Sons, and wondered if you wanted to go along."

Her smile looked even weaker than it had earlier. "Thanks, but I'll pass. I can't handle anything like a funeral home today. I'm not even sure how I'll handle it when the time comes for the service. But I really appreciate you inviting me along. You could be just shutting me out on all this."

"I guess. The detective said that, too, but I don't see how I could. It's not like most of this is your fault. Dennis pretended he was single while he was with you. He never even mentioned me. So it's not like you knew he was married." Besides, I figured her burdens were heavy enough right now; why dump more guilt on her that she couldn't do anything with? It was going to be hard enough for the young woman to deal with life in general. Her baby's father was dead and nothing could change that.

"Well, anyway, I appreciate it." Heather aimed the front seat vents at herself when the car started. "But this time, Gracie Lee, just take me home. I'll see you tonight at the chapel, okay?"

"Sounds like a plan." More of a plan, I thought, than I had to deal with Dodd and Sons once I got there. I imagined that this was going to be a strange situation even for them.

I was right about that one. The man dealing with me in his cool, pristine office looked young enough that he was probably part of the "and Sons" part of the funeral home business. His name was Scott, and he seemed hard-pressed to keep his jaw from hanging open as I explained what I could of the situation.

His eyes widened enormously as he shuffled paperwork on his desk. "Now let me get this straight. Your husband's body is being held by the coroner because he's apparently been murdered. There is one ex-wife involved in addition to yourself, and another woman and your husband's mother, who can't be found at this point. He has no life insurance that you're aware of and the business or businesses that he ran up until his…incapacitation may or may not have any assets."

It sounded even worse summed up like that. *Thanks a bunch, Scott.* "That's right. I'm positive, though, that his mother, once she does show up, would be appalled at the thought of him being buried by the county."

Scott's smile was rueful. "Well, I hate to tell you this, but the mere fact that you've shown up and made your whereabouts known before the body was released pretty much does in that notion. The county is off the hook once a legal next of kin appears, whether you like the deceased or not."

Lovely. My regard for Dennis dropped even more, what little there was to begin with. "I suspect that Dennis himself might have had resources squirreled away for emergencies, and I'm pretty sure that Edna does, too. We just can't find her at the moment."

"All right. Do you have any idea where any of these resources might be? And if you don't find them, how do you expect to pay for a funeral?" Poor Scott was getting paler by the minute.

"I can think of other places to look. And I haven't spoken with his ex-wife to see if she's aware of the existence of any life insurance policies on Dennis that he might not have shared with me." Although, given what I now knew about Dennis, I had to assume that he hadn't given any thought to what was going to happen to him after death. In the arena of spiritual concerns, he had put such thoughts off until another time or rejected them altogether. In the way of financial concerns, I suspected that death and burial were the furthest things from his mind. It was going to fall to those of us who were still here to deal with what Dennis had left us.

There was a computer screen on the corner of Scott's desk, so slim that it was hardly noticeable. He typed something in on the keyboard half-hidden on a tray jutting out from the desk and frowned. "Just on the off chance that there might have been something in the way of a prepaid plan, I typed in your husband's name. But unfortunately I don't see anything, Mrs. Harris."

"That would be part of the problem right there, Scott. To complicate the situation even more than I've already told you, my husband's last name is Peete," I told him, and spelled it for him. Nobody puts the last *e* on the end.

"Hmm." Scott was still frowning, but it was a different kind of frown this time. "There might be something after all. Definitely, there's a prepaid plan for an Edna Peete and she seems to have prepaid at least part of a plan for another individual. Mr. Peete's father wouldn't still be living, would he?"

"Not to my knowledge." It suddenly dawned on me that Dennis's father was something neither he nor Edna had ever mentioned in my presence. Once, long before we'd moved to California, Dennis had said something about growing up alone with his mom. But that was the sum total of what I remembered.

"Then if you're fortunate, there's already some provision made for your husband's burial. I can compare notes when the county releases the body, assuming that you tell them to send it here. Is that all right?"

It was as good an idea as anything else. Scott and I tied up what little we could, he gave me the traditional funeral director's limp handshake and I left.

Even Edna's house, empty as it was going to be, sounded pretty good at this point. It had been a long morning and a depressing one. I stopped by the grocery to pick up a few things to try and put together lunch for myself, and a few necessities for the next couple days. When I pulled into the driveway there was an older compact car parked on the street and a person parked in one of the two Adirondack chairs on the front porch.

When the stranger pulled himself out of the chair and rose, I had the odd thought, just for a moment, that somehow Ben had gotten out here to California. But no, it was a stranger, though he was definitely somebody in his teens or early twenties, with the tall, rangy gangliness of my son. This young man's hair was a shade or two darker than Ben's cinnamon and he was definitely dressed nicer than the ratty jeans and band T-shirts that Ben seemed to be favoring right now.

I got the car parked in the garage, but hadn't opened the door or managed to close the garage door before the young man was there beside the car. Up close he didn't look that much like Ben, but he didn't look like much of a threat of any kind, either. I still only opened my car door slowly, with a hand on my cell phone in case I needed to call 911 or something.

"Ms. Harris?" Okay, this was decidedly odd. I was so used to everybody I met in the past week calling me Mrs. Peete that somebody actually knowing or guessing who I was felt unsettling.

"Yes. Do I know you?" He didn't look familiar, but my stress level was high enough I wasn't sure that mattered.

"Not yet. My name's Sam Blankenship and I'm from the *Ventura County Star.*"

Great. The media had been alerted. In the back of my mind I'd been wondering about something like this ever since the detective said that Dennis's death had been ruled a homicide. When I thought about all the stories I'd seen in the local paper in the past six months about a suspicious death here or there, I knew that somebody would be calling eventually. Now, apparently, they had called.

That still didn't mean I had any idea what to do now. I should probably be dialing Fernandez on my cell phone, I thought. He wouldn't want me talking to a reporter, even one as young and basically harmless looking as this one. Still, part of this was a matter of public record, wasn't it? Surely I couldn't get into more trouble if I just stuck to the facts.

"Sam, I'd like to ask you kindly to get out of my garage. Go sit on one of those chairs on the porch again, and I'll come back out and talk to you in five minutes. I promise." He looked skeptical, but apparently Sam was still pretty new to this reporter business on a professional level because he didn't argue.

After a moment or two I won our staring contest and he headed out to the chairs on the porch. I closed the garage and went in the house for a minute to compose myself. Cub reporter or not, this was going to be a challenge. For the first time in a long time, my immediate response was prayer. With all the stuff facing me that was coming down, I figured I needed every scrap of help I could possibly muster.

7

When I went back to the porch I offered Sam coffee, which he declined. He looked more like somebody who'd drink one of those caffeinated power drink things, anyway. The funniest thing was that when I told him that, he totally blew away my perception of him. "Nope, no caffeine here, thanks. Not my thing."

A reporter who didn't do caffeine. It boggled the mind. "Okay. So how about orange juice or something?"

"Thanks, I'm cool." He opened a reporter's notebook that looked a lot like the one the detective carried. I was glad he hadn't pulled out a tape recorder, because I would have refused right away to talk to him. My head just wasn't together enough at this point for me to be comfortable with someone recording my words that accurately. "Okay, so let me make sure I have things straight so far. I came out to talk to you about the death of your husband, Dennis Peete. You are aware that his death has been ruled a homicide, right?" All I could do was nod and shrug.

"My notes say he passed away at the Conejo Board and Care last week when someone there apparently gave him a cup of liquid laced with an illegal substance. Is this correct?"

"So far it matches what I've been told or what I know." He might not look much older than Ben, but so far the kid was succinct and accurate.

"Do you or any of the rest of Mr. Peete's family plan any sort of lawsuit regarding the Board and Care?"

"Not at this time." I kept my voice as calm as possible, amazed that Detective Fernandez had let so little information out. Was it lying to let this young man think that there might be some involvement by the Board and Care in Dennis's death? It felt like a sin of omission, somehow, but not one I was willing to correct, either.

"Since there's no record of you having been arrested, Ms. Harris, I've got to assume the police don't think you had anything to do with your husband's death. Care to point me in the right direction?"

"No direction to point you in, Mr. Blankenship." Might as well keep things as detached as possible. It certainly couldn't hurt. "I'm just close enough to the investigation, at least the wrong end of it, that if the police have any theories they certainly aren't sharing them with me."

"Is there any chance I could speak with Mr. Peete's mother? I understand this is her house."

This kid was way too sharp. But then, he could have found that out a number of ways, from property records to a reverse directory that listed the names of owners of record of every business and home. After working in the offices at the community college back in Missouri, I knew a little bit about finding people just from having to track down students who failed to give us the right address. Back then it was usually a mixture of spaciness and the vague hopes their tuition bills might go astray. The ploy seldom, if ever, worked.

"This is her house, but she's not home right now." I didn't feel like sharing with him that she hadn't been home for a number of days. Another sin of omission. If there were a confession section of Christian Friends meetings, I was going to have a lot to tell them sometime in the near future. Maybe even tonight if I got a chance. "If you'll leave a business card, I can see that she gets it when I see her. I can't promise you anything, though, because I'm not sure when she's going to be back, and she's not big on communication."

"Okay. I'd appreciate it anyway," he said, fishing around in his jeans pocket and coming out with a business card. "I keep a few of these around for the folks that don't do e-mail."

"I imagine they're getting fewer and farther between these days," I said, mainly to make conversation.

"All the time. Even my grandmother has a Web site," he said with a grin. "Of course, I helped her set it up, but now she loads pictures and messages on it herself."

Even in my wildest dreams I couldn't imagine Edna uploading anything to a Web site. Still, she'd get a kick out of communicating that way. I made a mental note to push the computer literacy once she came back. Maybe

I could use the argument that she'd have more pictures of Ollie that way to show her seniors' group. Just thinking about it made me tear up a little. I was awfully tired of most of my life right now.

"I'm sorry to have to ask you all this," Sam said, apparently thinking that he was the one aggravating me. "But there's nobody else to ask, and I'm sure you're familiar with how little information the county sheriff's department funnels through their public information officer. And the medical examiner's office is even worse."

Knowing how tight-lipped Detective Fernandez was, I could imagine. "You have to do your job," I said, thinking that actually he could be a lot worse. And talking to him had let me know more about what the police were putting out than I'd known before.

"Yeah, but that doesn't always make it a pleasant job," he said, looking grimmer than I'd expect a young man his age to look. "Have Mrs. Peete call me when you can, will you?"

"I'll try my best," I promised, hoping that I'd get a chance to try soon. The longer that Edna was gone, the more I wondered about where she was hiding out. She'd left Dennis's bedside with nothing but her purse and the clothes on her back.

Just thinking about that made me wonder if that was still all she had. I didn't go back to the house for hours after Dennis died, so I assumed that Edna hadn't been back, either. I wasn't sure if a quick look through her closet or dresser drawers would tell me what, if anything was missing. I'd never done much of an inventory on what she wore, other than the fact that a lot of it seemed to be some shade of aqua.

Waving goodbye to the reporter, I tried to keep any and all of this thought process off my face, while inwardly urging him down the driveway so that I could go in and look in Edna's room. Once he pulled away I tried not to race back into the house.

Edna's room looked the same way it had the few times I'd been in it. Her furniture dated back to at least 1950 if not before—blond wood and a nondescript bedspread in ice-blue and—surprise!—aqua. On the wall near the dresser there were black-and-white baby pictures of someone I could only assume was Dennis, and a few knickknacks strewn on the top of the furniture.

The walk-in closet had a few hints that perhaps she'd been in here recently. There was a square indentation in the carpet that was empty now, as if a carry-on-sized suitcase normally rested there and was seldom moved. In among the neatly hung blouses, sweaters and polyester pants were several empty hangers, as if garments had been quickly pulled off and put in that missing suitcase. And to top things off, two of the different clear plastic containers that held her everyday shoes were empty. One at a time I could understand, but two empties meant Edna had been back here and packed.

This was definitely information I needed to share with Detective Fernandez. He wouldn't like hearing it and he might not even go along with my reasoning, but I owed it to him to let him in on what I'd found out.

Once I was sure that the reporter was long gone, I called the sheriff's department. I got Fernandez's voice mail, and debated on what to do. Would he appreciate the message, even if it wasn't given in person? It was hard to say. In the end I settled on giving him a shortened version of things.

"This is Gracie Lee Harris," I said, hating the way I sounded giving information to a machine. "I think there are some things missing from Edna's closet. I can't say how much, and when it might have happened. Just thought you should know." Hanging up, I felt a little silly. When I really analyzed what I'd told him, this didn't sound like much. As far as I knew, this could have been things that Edna had pulled together to give to the Salvation Army a month ago, not a hastily packed suitcase last week. Without knowing more about when things happened, and how, it certainly wasn't much to go on.

Still, there was at least a hint here that Edna had probably been back home, packed a bag and taken off. I resolved to tell Linnette and the rest of the Christian Friends that night when I went up to Conejo Chapel. They could help me sort things out, anyway.

There was no lack of help in sorting out that night. Paula had apparently decided to stay home, and nobody much minded. Linnette made plenty of coffee and even had cute little cookies that weren't chocolate chip. "They were in the grocery store bakery for Valentine's Day. That's why they're pink," she confessed, as she put them out on a plate on the coffee table. "Just because we're a week early, I figured that wasn't going to keep anybody from eating them."

"Definitely not," I told her, loading three of them onto a paper plate and adding cream to my coffee.

She gave me a stern look over her reading glasses. "That wouldn't happen to be dinner, would it?"

"Well, yeah." It was hard to get interested in food right now, alone in that house and with all the problems facing me. I hadn't counted on anybody catching me in the act, though.

"I want you to promise me that you'll plan regular meals tomorrow and the next day. You're in a rough situation right now, and if you neglect healthy eating it will just get worse," she lectured, sounding just like I knew my own mother would if she weren't two thousand miles away. Even Edna would never have let me get away with cookies and coffee for dinner.

"I'll do it. But it's such an effort right now."

She nodded. "I can just imagine. You still haven't figured out where Dennis's money went, right? And Edna hasn't shown up, either?"

"No, but remind me when the meeting gets under way that I actually have something to tell the group about that," I told her, as simultaneously Linnette's cell phone rang and Lexy came in shaking out a bright yellow jacket that looked like a stylish rain slicker.

"Wet out there again," she said, tossing her long blond hair like a cocker spaniel. "Sure ties up the 101. Oohh, cookies. Great." She picked up a few with the same gusto I'd shown. Having cookies for dinner seemed to be the common theme tonight.

Dot bustled in a moment later, closing down an umbrella with a handle shaped like a duck's head. It made me smile. Linnette was back, as well, motioning everybody to get their goodies and sit down. "That was

Heather on the phone and she's going to be a few minutes late. So let's get started and we'll catch her up when she gets here."

There were the prayers and opening statements about Christian Friends that sounded more familiar now. I especially liked the part that reminded us, Linnette looking over the rims of her reading glasses, that "what was said in this room stayed in this room," unless you got the permission of the others involved to do anything different. I felt like I needed friends close enough to really let go with right now, and this felt like the group to be that close with.

Dot gave a brief devotion. It was so good that I got a moment of panic wondering where on earth I'd find something like that if they ever asked me to do that. Maybe they had a grace period for newcomers. I hoped so. Then Linnette went around the group asking for specific concerns, warning me in advance that everybody else would get to go first since they hadn't had a chance last time.

"I'll start out myself, since I haven't said anything in a while. Actually I'm pretty stable. Both of the girls are doing well in school and work, and my job's been good. I'm on a reduced dose of meds and that seems to be keeping the demons at bay." Her reading glasses were put away now, and she looked over at me with the same kind, interested gaze she'd had most of the time I'd known her.

"I've been widowed about five years," she explained, "and it was rough at first handling everything that Tom and I used to together. Both girls were teenagers at the time of his death, and I didn't know how I was going to cope. Plus there were some other things I don't need to go into tonight. Let's just say I dealt with major depression, and it took me a good two years to find my way out of it.

"With the help of Pastor George, and a good doctor, life's a lot better now. Once I got through all this myself, the pastor thought I'd be a good leader for a Christian Friends group. I couldn't argue, seeing as how the group I was in at the time was what pointed me in the right direction to get my depression under control."

"And now she gets the rest of us under control instead," Dot quipped, a soft grin on her face. "Truthfully, though, you're a real inspiration, Linnette. We just don't say it often enough. Is there anything specific for us to keep you in prayer for?"

"Not right now. I just have to keep moving one day at a time. Although a relatively wealthy guy who wouldn't mind a forty-five-year-old with baggage couldn't hurt," she said, smiling back.

"I don't know. They always say to be careful what you pray for…." Dot let us fill in the blanks.

"That's true. I might get a whole different set of circumstances than I'm looking for," Linnette said. It was nice to hear her story, although I ached for her while she was filling me in. It made more sense now to know why she had so much insight into my situation; in some ways she'd been there herself. I hoped her husband hadn't been quite the same kind of guy Dennis was. That was pretty unlikely. Most middle-aged married guys seemed to be pretty boring sorts on the outside, at least.

Dot waved on the line of discussion when it came to her next. "Nothing big to talk about right now. Candace is good and likes her group home real well. Buck's busy on the computer when he's not out with the dogs. Life is pretty good."

She turned to me to fill me in on all that. Aside from Candace, whoever she was, none of it was news. "Candace is my daughter. She's thirty years old and I think the current politically correct term for her would be 'developmentally disabled.' I knew from the moment she was born that she had Down syndrome, but nobody told Candace, especially us, that it would keep her from doing things, so she did quite a bit. She holds down a simple job with a lot of help and support, and slowly but surely we have gotten less involved in her life."

"Which is quite an accomplishment when you think of everything you started out doing for her," Linnette added. "Dot and Buck have an apartment over their garage that Candace and a friend lived in for quite a while, just to give them some transition. Now she lives in Camarillo and comes home to visit and go to church on about the same schedule you'd expect from a mostly independent college student."

"And with the same amount of laundry," Dot said with a laugh. "I won't do it for her, but she sure likes using that machine at home that doesn't eat quarters like the one at the Laundromat."

Even tonight when she wasn't here, I wondered what possible problems brought Paula here. She didn't seem to have the same warm, outgoing bond with the group that most of the rest of these women did, but maybe she just had a prickly nature. Some people did, and I always felt sorry for them once I got over being aggravated by them, because I couldn't imagine going through life with that thin a skin.

I mean, I cry at the drop of a hat, but otherwise nothing much really bothers me, and I'd call myself easy to get along with. Maybe I was *too* easy to get along with, given that Dennis managed to pull everything he did on me. It was something to talk about here, once I got a chance. Right now it was Lexy's turn, and tonight she looked less like the savvy attorney than she had before.

She wore a soft sweater and worn jeans, and a bemused expression. "I've just had babies on the brain lately. Same old stuff, I guess. I know lots of people wait until their thirties to get pregnant and don't have any problems, but that sure hasn't been the case for us." She gave a deep sigh, and almost looked like a woman in her thirties for a change, instead of the perky cheerleader that I'd seen so far.

"Steve and I are trying to decide whether to get on the waiting list for a fertility specialist who practices at UCLA Med Center. It's so expensive, and I don't know if I could put him, or even myself, through half the stuff I know they'd probably want to do. But it's been four solid years of trying so far, and let's face it, I'm not getting any younger. Besides, the whole mindset is starting to affect my work."

"That's almost difficult for me to believe," Linnette said, looking a little startled. "You're usually more grounded than anybody else here."

"I know. But this week I pulled the ultimate female blooper." Lexy grimaced and took a drink from her water bottle. "I was visiting clients off-site in one of our satellite offices, and I ran into one of the women I don't see very often. I remembered that she had just told everybody she was expecting the last time I'd seen her. So she came into the office and I tell her, 'You look great. When's the baby due?' Apparently little Jaden is seven weeks old."

"Whoops," Dot said, trying to stifle a grin. "But I imagine we've all done that or something equally embarrassing at some time or another."

I knew I had. But that didn't make it feel any better for Lexy. The only thing that would have felt worse for most women was being on the receiving end of the question. I could just imagine the layer of frost that needed to be chipped out of that office before they got down to any other business.

"Jaden," Dot said, shaking her head and almost clucking. "What ever happened to ordinary names like Mary or Sue?"

"Jaden's a boy," Lexy said. "I'd never heard of it, either, but apparently it's hugely popular."

"We'll take your word on it," Dot said with a shrug. "Personally it's a new one on me, too." Before she could add anything else, Heather burst into the room. This time she wasn't dripping like she'd been the last time we had a meeting, but she was almost as dramatic.

Her wardrobe was beginning to suffer that assault most women's clothing dealt with in the last stages of pregnancy. Loose tops you were sure were going to fit for a while longer never did, and buying real maternity clothes seemed like a waste. Tonight she wore the same slightly baggy sweater she'd had on in the rain before, and another pair of bagged-at-the-knee leggings. This pair was gray. It was cool enough tonight that she was wearing tennis shoes instead of sandals, though. Unfortunately she had the same unhappy expression that she'd had previously.

"I'm so sorry I'm late. I really had everything ready to be on time, but then I got a phone call from that Detective Fernandez," she said, her lower lip starting to tremble. "He wants to see me tomorrow morning. I think I'm in trouble because he said that if I had a lawyer, it was probably time to bring one with me."

At least this time she wasn't throwing up. I decided that was a good thing, anyway. The fountain of tears that started after her announcement would be hard enough to calm down. It looked like another meeting where I might not get a chance to talk for quite a while.

That was okay, though, because this was a more serious problem even than the ones I was bringing with me tonight. Clearly something had happened that made Fernandez think that Heather was a viable suspect. The mere fact that this group of her churchgoing friends knew better wasn't going to convince him otherwise. We needed to come up with something else that looked a lot more like hard and fast proof to repute whatever it was that he thought he'd found.

Thankfully Lexy was there, and despite what she'd said before, she kept her wits about her. She might not have had the best week at work with the Jaden debacle, but she still proved her worth around here as a dynamite attorney. After getting Heather calmed down enough to talk, and asking her a few pointed questions, she was reassuring her that this wasn't the end of the world. I'm glad she could see it that way. It sounded pretty serious to me to have a county sheriff's detective tell you to bring a lawyer to the station, and I told her so.

Lexy actually smiled. "Hey, if he said that now would be a good time to bring a lawyer and that was as forcefully as he put it, he doesn't have anything that will stick for sure. That is the way he put it, right? Nobody Mirandized you or anything, right?"

Heather's blank looks had all of us who watched cop dramas on TV or read mystery novels explaining to her at once, along with Lexy. "Read you your rights, dear," Dot explained. "As in 'you have the right to remain silent' and all that."

"Oh. No, nobody did any of that. And he was still perfectly nice. He just sounded so serious."

Lexy nodded. "That probably means he has a witness of one type or another. There's either somebody that's seen you someplace you said you haven't been or somebody that thinks they can place you at or near the crime scene. They can't be real positive, because if they were you'd be on your way to a formal lineup by now. And if that were the case you'd have been told to lawyer up in a lot more forceful way. I wonder what he's got."

While she was puzzling it over, something hit me. I might be able to provide the missing piece of this particular puzzle. "There was someone of the housekeeping staff who might have seen who went in and out of Dennis's room just before he died," I said. I told them about Adela Rodriguez and what the detective had said about her before. I also added that in my other encounters with her, she didn't strike me as somebody who would make guesses about something as serious as murder.

Lexy smiled. "This helps, Gracie Lee. This really helps. Okay, who speaks the best Spanish?" The puzzled looks she got had her smiling even wider. "Hey, we can't all go down to the sheriff's station tomorrow with Heather like some kind of posse. I figure we'll have to leave a couple people behind. And if Ms. Rodriguez speaks mostly Spanish, then we need to understand what she says."

Dot waved a hand. "Even after all this time in Southern California, I'm afraid my Spanish is awful. Restaurant stuff mostly."

Heather smiled apologetically. "I'm with Dot. Besides, I don't think they'd let me stick around if they're interviewing a witness that they think saw me commit a murder."

Lexy looked at me and I shrugged. "I wish I could tell you otherwise, but I'm a Missouri girl, remember? I'm picking up a little already, but not enough to understand a native speaker, especially if she's excited."

Linnette put an arm around me. "You need to go anyway, because you're so involved in this. And I'll go with you to translate. One way or another I've picked up some great phrases in Spanish and I'm always looking for a way to try them out."

Lexy grinned. "And seeing as how you look more like an aging Valley girl than a *chica*, you can get away with things that another translator might not be able to."

Linnette's answering grin looked like a fox exiting the henhouse. "My thoughts exactly. Now what time tomorrow are we heading for the sheriff's department?"

8

Maybe if we spent enough time in the sheriff's department station I'd get used to it. I didn't know whether to hope I eventually did get comfortable there and finally stopped sweating every time the scent of the place hits my nostrils, or just hope I didn't have to go there again.

I'd have liked to think that I'd be done, soon, going to see Detective Fernandez about anything. But that would have meant that he either decided that Dennis's death was an accident after all, or figured out who did it, so it was not likely to happen anytime soon.

Today it still felt as uncomfortable as usual because nothing had changed. There were still a lot of folks in uniform behind glass partitions that I suspected were bulletproof windows that looked into offices and places to pay fines. Since they have some limited county holding cells down in the basement, there were plenty of noises and smells I associated with that, too, along with the vague scents of microwave popcorn and coffee floating around everyplace.

I had picked up Heather at her mother's house to take her to the station. We'd all agreed that in stressful situations like this one, she probably shouldn't drive. And I suspected that Lexy didn't want to have her stuck with a car there if the worst happened and they threatened to book her for something. I couldn't imagine the detective having any information that would result in that happening, but I'd been wrong before when it came to him.

Heather was shaky and nervous, but conversely looked better than I'd seen her in quite a while. She'd obviously dressed for the occasion in a pair of tailored slacks and a top that flattered her condition and her coloring. She even seemed to be wearing a touch of makeup and her hair was done. Maybe she was trying to make herself look as little as possible as she'd looked the day of Dennis's death, when we all had gravitated toward jeans and casual shirts except Edna. But then since Edna never wore jeans, it wasn't a rarity that she'd shown up that day in an aqua polyester pant suit. I wondered where she and her aqua wardrobe were spending their days right now. I had some ideas, but nothing I could prove so far.

Lexy met us in the parking lot, looking even more dressed up than Heather. "I'm going in to work after lunch," she said, conscious of our looks at her sharp outfit. For the most part I'd seen Lexy looking as casual as the rest of us in the evenings at Christian Friends meetings, but that didn't appear to be how she went to work. "And I talked to one of my friends from law school.

If this goes any further than today she's on board to represent you. If anything happens, you don't want an entertainment lawyer handling your case for a criminal matter."

"I trust you, Lexy," Heather said, her voice sounding a bit shaky.

"That's a real compliment, but I don't trust me, not in a case like this could become. But for today, I think I'll be fine. And with me along, it will be obvious to this detective that you took him seriously."

I didn't think that would be a problem. Fernandez expected all of us to take him seriously, and the rest had so far. I even had most of the time, even though today it was harder to take him seriously than it had been before. How could he possibly believe that Heather had murdered Dennis? It just didn't make sense to me. But then, the entire situation we'd found ourselves in here didn't make sense to me anymore.

When we all trooped down to the detective division, I noticed something important enough to try and catch Lexy's eye. I couldn't, not right at first. So as she walked down the hallways and waiting areas in front of Linnette and myself and as she chatted with Heather, she didn't know what I'd seen.

Or rather *who* I'd seen. The slender, older Latina blended right in sitting on the benches with a younger friend or relative, both of them in the area I'd associated so far with family visiting for the jail. That, or it was where you went to bail somebody out when they were in the county lock-up cells beyond the heavy doors nearby. I thanked Ben silently for being a fine, upstand-

ing young man of such good character that I hadn't ever
had to find out what the similar facilities looked like in
Missouri. As it was, I could only guess about why people were sitting on those benches. Judging from the demeanor of the people sitting there, none of their reasons
were happy ones.

The one woman with neat but slightly faded
clothes, a narrow face and dark hair going silver was
definitely Adela Rodriguez from the care center,
though. I'd not known her name until Detective Fernandez told me, but I recognized her easily, even without the uniform she usually wore. When she saw our
group, she sat up straighter and said something in a
very low tone to the younger woman sitting beside
her.

That was the moment I was positive that by marching
Heather past her, we were providing an unofficial lineup
for Fernandez and his main witness. I didn't know
whether to say something out loud to Lexy and Heather
ahead of us or not, so I kept quiet.

Jeannie in the detective division's front office seemed
surprised to see this big a group. Even before all four of
us got comfortable in the outer office she'd buzzed back
to the detective and he was coming through the door.
"Why don't you go ahead and take care of that other matter for me," he said to her, and she rose and nodded. I
suspected that the "other matter" had something to do
with alerting Adela outside, and I felt like telling him
she'd already seen us go in one direction up the hallway.

"Ms. Taylor, it looks like you brought quite a group,"
he said, surveying us.

"Well, you said to bring my lawyer, and I couldn't see leaving Gracie Lee out of this," she said, not really explaining Linnette's presence. I was glad she hadn't. Fernandez wasn't going to be overly thrilled if he figured out how much conniving we'd done the night before.

"Alexis Adams," Lexy said, sticking out a hand for a handshake. "I really hope my presence here won't be necessary, Detective."

"I'm sure we all do, Ms. Adams," he said with a disarming smile. "For the present I can guarantee you that your presence isn't really needed because the first thing I need to do is ask Ms. Taylor to go back down to the fingerprinting station where she's been before. It seems we had a small problem with the card she left last time."

Lexy and Heather both looked slightly confused and annoyed. I was pretty sure that the card I'd watched them use to print Heather last time was just as good as any of the others we'd left. However, when I thought about it a moment more, I figured out what Fernandez was doing. Going from here to the fingerprinting station would require another stroll right past the bench where Adela and her companion sat.

"Do you need mine, as well, Detective? My prints were taken during the same session that Ms. Taylor's were. If there was a problem…" I let things trail off, wondering if he'd hesitate.

"No, they seem to be fine, thanks," he said breezily. "There's no need for you to keep her company. I'll walk her down there if you like while you wait here with Ms. Adams."

Lexy began to protest, but cut herself short and waved Heather on when she apparently caught the message I was trying to send her without speaking. Once Heather and Fernandez were out of the room she came closer to where Linnette and I stood. "All right, explain."

"I'm pretty sure I know what this is all about. When we were coming to the office here, I spotted the care facility staff member I told you about. If anybody had seen who went in and out of Dennis's room in the fifteen minutes or so that really matter, it would have been her."

"Ah. And something she's said really did make the detective think it must be Heather. But as we decided last night, it can't be a real good look she got at whoever this was, and she can't be sure it was Heather. I'd have to guess that means she saw the back of whoever she saw, or a real quick view otherwise."

"Makes sense," Linnette said. "I might just mosey up the hallway and see what's going on. Maybe even fix my lipstick in the ladies' room nearest that hallway."

I was dying to go with her, but that was going to be way too obvious. For now I needed to stay away from that bit of action, as far away as Heather did. If Fernandez had any suspicions that Heather could possibly be guilty, we didn't want to fan the flames. "Hurry back," I told her. "It's going to be a long wait until we hear something."

"Wonder how the detective will feel about us using this office to pray in," Lexy said. "Because I don't know about you, but I think that's the best use of our time." I couldn't agree with her more, so we prayed very quietly together as long as everyone else was gone.

* * *

By the time Linnette made her way back to the detectives' waiting area, she looked like the cat that ate the ca-
nary instead of a woman who just fixed her lipstick.

"That took longer than any makeup-fixing I've ever
seen," I told her. I'd about prayed myself out, and started
on a little worrying for good measure, by the time she
came back. I knew it was foolish, and my time would have
been better spent praying some more. Knowing it and
doing it, however, are still two different things with me.
At least I can recognize when I'm falling down on the job
now, anyway. I figure it's a start in this faith-walk business.

"I think we're okay," she said. Heather was sitting
down, having gotten tired of pacing around the room.
"And I don't think Lexy is going to have to call that
friend of hers." She sat down and patted Heather on the
arm. "This is all going to work out."

"What makes you say that? It has to be something
good for you to be smiling that much," I said, sitting
down on the other side of Heather where I could hear
whatever Linnette had to say to her.

"While I was in the ladies' room, the woman you
pointed out to us earlier came in with her friend and
without her police escort. Even Jeannie the receptionist
wasn't with them. So I slipped into a stall and closed the
door where I could overhear what they were saying without them watching me. They talked for several minutes,
and I'm pretty sure that Señora Rodriguez is certain that
you're not the person she saw."

"What did she say?" Heather asked. She looked limp
with relief.

"Just be glad you've kept yourself up while you're expecting this baby, honey." Linnette patted her arm again. "According to the detective's main witness you have too *pequeño* a *nalgas* to be the person she saw."

"What?" Heather and I said in chorus.

Linnette grinned again. "You look too skinny from the back. She's pretty sure that the person she saw coming out of Dennis's room was a pregnant woman, and she's almost positive that the lady in question was blond, or at least had light-colored hair. But whoever she saw, her, uh caboose was wider than yours, Heather."

"And that's not something I could have changed in a week, for sure. At least not from wider to skinnier at this point in my life," Heather said, smiling herself now.

"Funny, that's just what Señora Rodriguez and her companion, who seems to be her daughter-in-law, were saying."

Detective Fernandez probably thought we'd all finally gone the rest of the distance around the bend when he came into the waiting room and we were all giggling with our heads together. But then, he didn't have high expectations from our sanity to begin with—except maybe about Linnette—so perhaps it wasn't a problem.

He definitely looked like he'd expected other news from his witness. The tightness around his face was back, making him look again like a man with a perpetual migraine. Lexy, walking a little bit behind him, was smiling as broadly as she dared.

"Thank you for coming down so promptly to redo your fingerprints, Ms. Taylor. And I appreciate you bringing your attorney, even though it appears that isn't going to be necessary after all. If I have any more questions for any of you, I'll call you. You're free to go." He said that last sentence with a finality that made it sound more like "and get out of here before I change my mind."

None of us appeared ready to challenge him on that part. We were all out in the parking lot standing at Lexy's car talking before we knew it.

Lexy hugged Heather and said goodbye to the rest of us. "I ought to get moving and get to the office while I'm still in the gap between rush hours."

"Thanks for doing this. I don't know what would have happened without you here," Heather said, her lower lip trembling a little.

"I'm just glad I didn't have to do much of anything. I haven't done any criminal work to speak of, and I'd hate to think of using you for a guinea pig," Lexy told her.

"So go do what they pay you to do," Linnette said, motioning toward her car door. "We'll make sure that Heather gets home all right, and I'll head to work myself. Gracie Lee, do you need us to do anything as a group before the services for Dennis?"

I honestly hadn't thought about that before this moment. "Let me think about it. If nothing else, I could probably use some backup at the family hours beforehand, whenever we work that out. I really need to talk to Carol and see if she and the rest of his family had anything in mind." For that matter, I needed to see if Carol had any hints as to where some of his family was at this point. Edna, in particular, came to mind. "I'll call you tonight or tomorrow morning," I told her.

Linnette nodded and I looked back at the building. I hadn't talked directly to the detective about Edna's clothing being gone from her closet. "Could you take Heather home for me? I forgot to tell Detective Fernandez one last thing."

"Sure, no problem. Call me when you need me." A quick hug and Linnette and Heather were gone, too, leaving me heading back into the building. It might not have been the brightest move I'd made all day, but it needed to be done. Now why did that feel like it could have been the motto for my life in the past two weeks?

Jeannie didn't look too pleased to see me this quickly again when I got to the detective division waiting room and asked for Fernandez. "He's got somebody in his office right now," she said. "I think they're going to be in there a while. Maybe it would be better if you came back another time."

"It would be helpful if I didn't have to come back," I told her. "I had several things to tell him."

She didn't offer much more and I tried to decide how much more to say myself. "Maybe I could go down the street somewhere close and grab a cup of coffee and come back. Do you think that would work?" I would really have rather parked myself right here in the lobby and watched him walk out with Adela Rodriguez, which was what I expected would happen, but that would probably make him unhappy. The last thing I needed right now was an unhappy police officer to add to the rest of my problems, especially when he'd just had to give up the idea of somebody else as his prime suspect in my husband's murder.

"I imagine that would work. Do you know of a place to go?" Jeannie seemed more than ready to get rid of me.

"I'm not as familiar with this neighborhood as I am some other places." And I didn't particularly want to be, since my main association with this neighborhood was the sheriff's department. But Jeannie directed me to a nearby family-run coffeehouse and bakery and I spent a while there sipping a latte and wondering if Fernandez was done with talking to the witness yet.

After twenty minutes, I hoped that he was, because there was only so much time I was willing to spend trying to ignore a well-stocked bakery case. In five more minutes I was back in the sheriff's department parking lot. My patience was rewarded by seeing Adela Rodriguez come out of the building with her daughter-in-law, both of them still talking to each other in hushed tones as they made their way to an older sedan and got in.

Jeannie seemed much happier to see me when I came back to her desk. That just confirmed my suspicions that before, she was getting me out to avoid Adela. She rang Fernandez, and in a matter of seconds, he breezed out of the back room and ushered me into his office. "Jeannie said you'd asked to speak to me a little while ago. I appreciate your coming back," he said. "I've got a fair amount of cases right now and something came up that I couldn't wait to deal with."

Oh, that was too much. If he'd just said he wouldn't discuss the case with me and gone on I would have understood. But to pretend something else was going on was trying patience that I didn't really have right now. I felt like I usually did when Ben was trying to give me a line about why he was late making curfew or why a particular grade wasn't what I thought it should be and he, usually, knew it could be if he'd just studied. I felt, in other words, like I was being fed a line.

Counting to ten didn't do anything. I was still just as mad as I'd been before. "Detective, I'll level with you. I saw Adela Rodriguez out there when we came in this morning and I have a fair idea of why Heather was called back in here. And I have to figure that something about Ms. Rodriguez's identification of Heather as a suspect didn't work out or you would not have let Heather leave earlier. So please, don't try to tell me that you're busy with other cases. Although I'm sure you have plenty to do with this case and the others you have to be handling right now." It was as nice as I could possibly be and be honest right now. At least I didn't go into the details of how I knew for certain that Adela Rodriguez hadn't seen Heather leaving that room.

The detective didn't appear to know what to say to me. His expression wavered between confusion and one I'd seen before that I would have called consternation. "You know, I didn't say I was busy with another case, just that I was busy. And none of this is really your business—" he started before he cut himself off.

"I think it is, at least to a degree. After all, it's my husband who was murdered. And you can't deny that I was probably your first suspect. I know that statistically if a serial killer or some other total stranger doesn't kill you in this country, your nearest and dearest family probably did."

He shrugged. "That's truer than not, usually. But nothing's going to be helped by my telling you the details of this murder investigation, especially when you're so free with what I tell you."

So free with what he told me? I hardly knew anybody in California, so it was difficult to figure out what he meant and I told him so. He got all argumentative looking again on me. "Ms. Harris, you're best buddies with your late husband's fiancée, which still has me so confused I can't figure out up from down on this one. I can't understand why you weren't the one pushing for me to file some kind of charges against her from the first moment."

"Because she didn't do it," I said, without even thinking. It didn't take much thought to say that, because something—call it intuition or whatever—had convinced me from the first that Heather was innocent in this particular situation. "She may have a lot of problems, Detective, the least of which being that she's out over six thousand dollars to the same con man that took thirty thousand from me and duped both of us into believing we were the only woman in his life and he loved us madly. The funny thing about that is that Dennis was so convincing that he may have believed that part himself."

His soft brown eyes were clouded. "Still, it takes two to tango, as the old saying goes. Don't you have any hard feelings against her?"

"Hard feelings? Yes, of course I have hard feelings, because I'm human. She's younger and prettier than I am and pregnant with my husband's child. But 'hard feelings' are a long way from suspecting she murdered Dennis, or wanting her prosecuted for it. Does that make any sense to you?" I was beginning to wonder if it did, because we'd had similar conversations to this one now several times. My logic and his just didn't seem to be in the same ballpark.

"Maybe. And I'm pretty sure that wasn't what you came back here to discuss with me. At least I hope it wasn't."

He was giving me a way to get off the subject gracefully and for a change I took it. He'd had a point earlier when he said he hadn't ever told me he was busy with another case, and I probably had lit into him unfairly this time. "You're right. I need to talk to you about what I found at home. I wish it were something more concrete, but I think it's worthwhile, anyway." I went into more detail than I had before about the dents in Edna's closet floor carpeting and the missing clothing. The detective's expression was a little skeptical, but he wasn't arguing, either.

"It's a possibility," he said. "I'll agree with you, I wish there was more proof of what you're suggesting. As is, we don't really have enough evidence yet to file a missing-person report, much less suspect foul play. She's a sane, healthy adult who doesn't really have anybody else to answer to. None of us like the fact that she appears to have walked out of her son's room at a critical time and disappeared, but there's not a thing we can do about it."

That about summed everything up. I wished there was more that Fernandez could do toward pressuring somebody into telling what they knew about Edna. I still had the feeling that Carol and Becca knew more than they were letting on.

"Maybe when we're able to set a date for the funeral services, and can actually run an obituary in the paper that says something definitive about services, she'll turn up." It was my best hope, but I had to admit it wasn't a real strong one.

"That should be soon. The medical examiner's office called me this morning and said that they may be able to release the body by the end of today, or tomorrow morning. I didn't have any new tests for them to run, and everything we've ordered so far is complete. I'll let you know as soon as I hear something. And in the meantime—"

"I know. Don't leave town. Which is a little ridiculous because I have far too much to do to leave town even if I wanted to." I was a little too edgy and tired to be terribly polite at this point.

That was a mistake, because in a heartbeat Fernandez was in my face and in a real mood. "Look, I wish you'd listen to me. Despite what you think, I'm not considering you a suspect here. You haven't put all the pieces together in this mess or you'd be a lot more grateful to me and the rest of the sheriff's department, and a lot more willing to do what I'm telling you instead of sticking your nose where it doesn't belong."

"What do you mean?" The intensity of his speech scared me. He obviously believed what he was telling me, but I wasn't sure why he was so upset.

"Oh, forget it." He seemed to regret that he'd said anything. "I should know better than to say anything, but, lady, you're driving me nuts."

"Why? Because I'm not providing you with a nice, neat package all tied up to solve my husband's murder?

Because despite what you think, I can't hate the younger woman he was obviously planning to run off with?"

"No. Because you won't sit still and let us do our job. And part of that job is keeping you safe, Ms. Harris, because somebody's tried to kill you twice now and may just well try again."

None of my body parts worked right all of a sudden. Everything felt cold and stiff and there was this funny ringing hum in my ears. "Kill me? But…no. That can't be right. It was Dennis who got run off the road to begin with."

The detective sighed. "In *your* car, headed toward *your* house. And then when that didn't work, somebody fed him poison out of a cup that only *you* had been drinking out of previously. There are at least four sets of prints on that cup, but on the inside the only evidence that someone's been drinking from it comes from your mouth."

I felt like passing out or throwing up or something. He was right, I'd never thought about that part before. And I didn't really want to think about it now. Besides my new friends at the chapel, I was two thousand miles from anybody who cared about me. And apparently, a whole lot closer to somebody who wanted me dead.

I must have turned as pale as I felt. The detective put a steadying hand on my arm. "I've said way too much here, and it's probably just my cop's way of thinking anyway." Fernandez was backpedaling, but it wasn't working. The expression on his face told me he regretted what he'd said, but his eyes said that it was the truth.

"I won't leave town," I said, trying to make my voice sound stronger than I felt. "And I'll make sure somebody I trust knows where I am all the time."

"I hope that includes me," he said, still looking grim. "Because right now, I'd have to say there aren't too many people around here you can fully trust. Whether they were aiming for you in the first place or for him, someone killed your husband, Ms. Harris. And we still don't know who."

"I'll keep that in mind, Detective. In the meantime I need to go over to Conejo Community Chapel and let the staff there know that I'm going to take them up on their offer to help with a funeral for Dennis. Thanks to the folks at the chapel, I've remembered where else besides your department to put my full trust."

His face clouded a little again. "That's your choice, Ms. Harris. I can't say that I share that trust, but you go right ahead." I went out to the parking lot where it took me several tries to get the key into the ignition and start the car so that I could head toward the chapel. I tuned the radio to the one Christian station I could receive. I needed a little more reminder of just where that trust was coming from.

9

Of course I went straight to someone I could pour my heart out to. "Have you thought about a job?" Linnette was looking over her reading glasses at me as we sat at our familiar table at the Coffee Corner. As usual, I was drinking decaf because my nerves didn't need any more caffeine with all the other problems I had going on.

"Definitely. I've got to do something to keep from going nuts, and just to have some money coming in for a while. There's precious little in my account, and the longer that Edna's gone, the less I can figure out about what to do about the household expenses." Bills would start to come soon for utilities and services that she usually paid, and I certainly didn't want the electricity or the phone cut off. With Ben and my mom so far away, the computer and the telephone were my lifelines right now.

"I think you'd more than qualify for some of the work-study stuff that the university has open. Not everything they suggest for graduate students involves teaching, you know."

Actually, I didn't know. Until recently I hadn't thought about who all these people were in places like Linnette's bookstore and the coffee shop where we sat drinking our lattes, but it made sense that many of them were probably students. "Do you have anything open in the store?" It would suit me as well as anything, and give me a chance to see my friend.

Linnette shook her head. "Not right now, but I'm pretty sure that there's something open here at the coffee shop. There almost always is. If you want me to ask Maria when she comes in, I'll be happy to."

"Please." It was the most mindless job I could imagine, for the most part, which would be right up my alley at the present. I didn't think I could handle anything too far up the ladder from mindless with everything else going on in life.

"I will. And I have to tell you that I'm more than a little concerned about the rest of what you've shared." It hadn't taken me long once I'd gotten there to tell her all about Fernandez's dire warnings. "Do you really think he's right, and that someone was out to get you instead?"

I swirled my drink around in the cup, staring at the pale foam on top. "It's possible. It was my car that Dennis was driving the night of his accident, and he normally never drove it. No one looking out for him would have expected him to be driving that car unless they'd followed him all the way from Heather's."

Linnette nodded, looking worried. "And we know that nobody who was there that last day expected him to be drinking out of your teacup, or anything else."

I'd been thinking about that one even more than the car. "Not when they dropped the drugs in the cup, for sure. Unless it was someone on staff, and that hardly seems likely."

"According to what the police have told us so far, anyway." Linnette looked over her reading glasses at me again. "I want you to be careful, Gracie Lee."

"I'm being as careful as possible. It is scary. But there's not much more that I can do about it. Plus there are so many things I have to do about Dennis's funeral arrangements. I have a feeling Pastor George is going to regret the warm, open nature of the Community Chapel once I start pestering him."

Linnette shook her head, making those deep red waves of lush hair bounce. "Not for a moment. That's what he's there for. And that's what groups like Christian Friends are there for, too. Don't do any of this alone unless you want to, okay?"

"Okay. And I appreciate you asking Maria about a job when she comes in. I'll either call you later or drop back by once I've gone by the chapel." And with that I put a lid on my cooling latte and went on to the harder errands I needed to do. It was good to be bolstered with coffee and friendship when the going got rough. And the going had gotten plenty rough lately.

I ran out of coffee before I ran out of rough going as I sat in Pastor George's office and explained everything that I could to him. Fortunately he was used to difficult situations and kept several boxes of tissues around the office for just such occasions.

Looking into his lined middle-aged face I got the feeling that there probably wasn't a thing I could have told him that would have shocked or surprised him. "I guess you've heard it all after a few years as pastor of a good-size church," I said, trying to stop from crying.

"Let's just say I've heard a great deal of what causes people pain in this world. And being a quarter-century past divinity school doesn't hurt, either. There are things that would have left me speechless at twenty-eight that I can at least breathe through now." He had a nice smile, a little sad around the edges, with kind gray eyes. I would have loved to have done something about the unfortunate comb-over he wore, but if that was the worst fault I ever found in this man, I'd be okay.

For someone who had solved her own problems for close to forty years I sure felt like I'd turned into a needy, hopeless sort in the past two weeks. But then, the kind of problems I'd solved before were child's play compared to discovering that my husband had a pregnant fiancée, or finding out that somebody was apparently trying to kill me but got him instead, and then succeeded in killing him after all. And that didn't even touch the money issues, or dear, missing Edna.

"Well, I appreciate you being able to breathe through everything I've told you today. If you want to withdraw the offer that Linnette had made for someone from here to officiate at the funeral at Dodd and Sons, I'd certainly understand."

He shook his head. "I wouldn't dream of it. I can certainly preach at a funeral without approving of everything the deceased did in his life. Funerals are really more for the living relatives and friends who attend them. I can't do anything for Dennis at this point. What I can do is give comfort to those who attend his funeral while making them aware of the love God extends to all of us in His son. Sometimes I feel that occasions like this are the ones that allow me to really flex my faith muscles."

I hadn't thought of things in anywhere near that context before, and told him so. He smiled again. "Now, do we have a timetable for all of the final arrangements yet?"

"Not quite. Once I get a call from Detective Fernandez I'll know when Dennis's body will be released. It will go directly to Dodd and Sons, where I've already spoken to Scott. After that there will be at least two or three days of preparation, so I'm figuring that nothing will happen before Friday at the earliest."

I sat looking at the small notepad on which I'd scribbled a to-do list of things to discuss. "I still have to talk to Dennis's former wife, Carol. I want to at least offer her and their daughter a chance to be involved in as much of this as possible. I imagine she'll turn down the offer but his daughter, Becca, might accept." After my limited contact with the angry young woman, it was hard to say.

Pastor George and I agreed to stay in touch, and he walked me out into the main office to introduce me to the church secretary, whose name was Helen, and explain to her what was happening. Helen, a woman with a tight silver perm, didn't look a lot younger than Edna. She wasn't any more easily rattled than her boss, though, because she took down everything he told her with brisk efficiency and never batted an eye. If multiple-family funerals were a new concept for her, she didn't show it. We talked about bulletins for the service for Dennis, and came to the conclusion there wasn't much Helen could do this far ahead of time. I left there feeling as if I'd gotten something accomplished, even though it wasn't a huge something. The way my days had been going lately, *any* sense of accomplishment was a good thing.

I needed to accomplish something even more intense pretty soon, but I needed fuel before doing it. So I stopped by the quiet, empty house and made myself a quick lunch. I'd never been one for keeping the radio or TV on all the time, but it was getting to be a habit while I was here alone. Otherwise the silence was almost creepy.

For the first time, as I ate, I really thought about the future. The immediate future was pretty unpredictable. I couldn't tell what I'd be doing in the next week or so, other than some time we'd have services for Dennis. Maybe Edna would show up, and maybe she wouldn't. I'd have to talk to a lawyer soon to figure out what kind of legal proceedings I needed to start to determine if there was any way to get my money back from Dennis's virtually nonexistent estate. I needed to find at least a part-time job—whether it was at the coffee shop at school or somewhere else—and go back to my studies.

On top of all that, I really had to start thinking about moving to another place. If Edna didn't come home soon I didn't have much real right to stay here now that Dennis was gone. And if she did come back in the next few days the situation would feel even more awkward. Dennis, even uncommunicative in a hospital bed, had been the only tie between the two of us. Now that he was gone, there wasn't much of anything to sustain a relationship. This was no Ruth and Naomi situation. I suspected we'd both be more than ready to move on from each other.

I needed more time to think than the few minutes it took to finish a sandwich and a few potato chips. Even peeling and sectioning an orange and eating it slowly afterward, I ran out of food long before I ran out of questions. So I combed my hair and made sure I had lipstick on again and checked my maps. It was time for a little drive.

I found Carol Peete's house in Woodland Hills without much problem. It was a middle-class community in the San Fernando Valley full of modest two-story and ranch homes with small but neatly manicured lawns and a lot of strip malls along the main streets. Other than the palm trees and bougainvillea in the front yards, you could have been in any suburban area I'd ever seen. There were lots of SUVs and pickup trucks, and now that it was midafternoon I noticed that a couple of ten- or twelve-year-old boys in the neighborhood were dragging out a plastic ramp and working on their skateboard tricks.

At first I'd planned to call and give Carol a lot of warning that I'd be visiting her, but then decided it would just give her more time to reject my visit. So I'd driven almost to her neighborhood, pulled into a shopping center and looked up the phone number, calling from my cell phone. She'd sounded surprised and not terribly encouraging but said I could come by if I didn't plan on staying long, or mind dealing with her grandson. Since I was anxious to see the baby, anyway, I agreed. Ten minutes later I was in front of her tan stucco house, watching the neighbor kids set up their ramp.

When Carol Peete opened the door I had one of those moments where I had a great realization. Dennis had spent his life working his way through a succession of the same type of woman. I wondered if there were any others out there we didn't know about, falling between her age and mine, and then Heather and me on the other end. Otherwise if you could line us up it would have looked like a family reunion of some sort. We might not have looked as similar as sisters, but we could definitely all three have been cousins.

Carol had light brown hair, a little bit darker than mine, just as mine was darker than Heather's. The first Mrs. Peete had helped hers along a little with some highlights or streaks, which probably covered up a little gray. Her bone structure was similar to mine, and what I expected Heather's would be if she weren't eight months pregnant by now. We could all stand to lose maybe ten pounds under normal circumstances, and were what a polite woman would call "well endowed" in the chest region. Right now Carol wore jeans and a sweater, and had answered the door in bare feet, with a laughing blond baby on her hip as an accessory.

"Hi, I'm Gracie Lee."

"I figured as much. You know I'm Carol. Come on in. Like I said, I can't promise you much time. If this guy starts one of his screaming fits, we won't be able to hear each other, anyway. Fortunately he's good-natured most of the time. Takes after his father, thankfully." She had a brief look that said she couldn't believe she'd said that, but I let it pass.

I followed her through the front hall, which separated a small formal living room and dining room. We went back to the kitchen where windows opened into a sunny expanse of pool deck and well-planted but small backyard typical of Southern California homes.

"This is Ollie?" I waved at him, figuring he was probably at that age where he wouldn't have anything to do with a stranger, even one that looked slightly like his grandmother. He was smiling right now and gumming on something that looked like it had started life as part of a stale bagel. After what she'd said about his screaming fits, I didn't want to make him unhappy.

"It is. Does this mean that you and Becca have actually talked long enough for you to know his name?" Carol had an inquisitive look in her tired gray eyes. She motioned me to a seat at her kitchen table, which I took gratefully.

"We've talked, although not since the day Dennis died. And mostly she talked about Ollie, how old he was, that he was teething a lot. I wish Dennis could have gotten to know him. He looks like a great kid." He did—a nice, solid healthy baby with little squiffs of blond hair standing up in fine cowlicks.

"Yeah, well, from what I've heard he was too busy starting another generation to be bothered with grandkids even before meeting Ollie became a nonissue." Carol poured herself a cup of coffee and held the pot up in question, to which I asked for a cup. She got out another ironstone mug and poured. It was good and strong and black when I retrieved it from the counter. I didn't want her carrying it with Ollie on one hip, and he didn't want to be put down.

"You may be right there. I just found out about Heather a little while ago myself."

"Did it surprise you?" Whatever Carol was, shy wasn't part of the equation. I guess she couldn't have been and dealt with Dennis for this many years.

"It did. I had suspected something was up, but I figured whatever had happened was business related, not another woman. I guess I just hadn't considered that."

"Because he was attentive and flattering when he was around, and you felt like you were the only woman in the world when he looked into your eyes." She was dancing Ollie in her lap now, and there was an odd difference between her flat, practiced tone of voice and the shining love for this beautiful child that came through in her gaze.

"You're right. You've thought about this a lot, haven't you?"

"Too many times. I'm over Dennis and I have been for a number of years. I'm sorry he's dead, I guess. If nothing else, it means that Becca will never get the last of her college tuition money back. She's still paying off the loans, and will be for years. Once her father 'invested' the money her grandmother had put aside for her, there wasn't anything anywhere for her to go to school on. No surprise there, considering it was Dennis." She looked over the bouncing baby. "I won't even ask you how much he took you for."

It shook me for a moment that she hadn't questioned for a moment if Dennis had gotten money from me. I wish I'd talked to her quite a while ago. Maybe a lot of things would have turned out differently. Or maybe not. She was right about another thing—Dennis was always so persuasively charming that no one else bad-mouthing him would have made a difference.

"Thanks. I appreciate the candor. Let's just say I'm missing some money and leave it at that. I actually came by to discuss funeral service plans. I want to involve you, and Becca, to whatever extent you want to be involved. I expect to know before noon tomorrow when the services will be. I already know where—at Dodd and Sons in Rancho Conejo."

Carol leaned forward, still holding the baby. "Does this mean you've talked to Edna?" She looked like she wanted to take the question back the moment she asked it.

"No, why? Do you know where she is?"

There was a pause before she answered while she paid attention to Ollie, brushing nonexistent crumbs off the front of his blue sleeper.

"Of course not. But once a few years back she'd mentioned having a prepaid plan there, and that Dennis had talked her into cosigning on something that paid for him, too. Not that he ever expected to use it, of course. But if there was a way for somebody else to pay for something…"

That sounded like the Dennis I was coming to know after his death. I'd probably known most of these things before, but hadn't been in a place to accept them. Carol

Peete had had much more time alone with her thoughts of Dennis than I had. "You're sure she hasn't contacted you or Becca? I'm getting pretty worried about her. She hasn't ever mentioned anyplace else she'd go—no other family or anything. And she's been gone more than a week."

"Don't look at me. We have been barely on speaking terms for years. If we've met at all, you can guarantee that the reason for getting together has been this little man here. She loves him, of course. And Becca would be her favorite grandchild even if she wasn't her only grandchild, just for producing a beautiful male child."

"That's interesting. She only had nice things to say about you the whole time I lived with her."

Carol shrugged, her eyes looking even more tired. "Of course. I wasn't there." This whole afternoon was becoming a learning experience for me in ways I hadn't expected. In the past few months when I'd been listening to Edna, I'd felt like nothing I was ever going to do would measure up to Carol. It seemed that Edna had played that same trick on all of us. Maybe that was why she'd warmed up to Heather so much the day Dennis died. Perhaps she saw another chance for bonding with a new listener, one that might be another shot at a male grandchild.

Ollie was beginning to rub his eyes, which made him even fussier when gummy bits of the bagel he'd been munching embedded themselves into his pudgy cheeks and pale eyebrows. When he finally threw away the chunk of bagel and gave a shout of frustration, I figured the interview was close to over.

"He's not going to last much longer," Carol said with a practiced look. She stood up and put him in my lap while he was still facing her, so the baby wouldn't be immediately aware of who had him. "I know he's going to crab, but would you hold on to him a minute? I need to get a fresh diaper and a couple other things before I settle him down."

"Sure." I'd never argue with holding a baby, even one who was a bit fussy. He arched his back so that I had to struggle to hold on to him while he fishtailed in my lap. I knew that turning him around toward me would probably result in howls, but he'd be easier to handle facing me. The moment I turned him, his lip quivered and he started whimpering. "I know. But Grandma will be back in just a minute. It will be okay, Ollie." He didn't go into a full-fledged fit, for which I was thankful. And aside from the crying, it was wonderful to hold him. He was warm and cuddly, and his hair still smelled a little like baby shampoo. Of course it smelled a little like wet bagel, too, but that was to be expected in a busy guy his age.

Had it really only been seventeen years since Ben was this small? It felt more like a hundred, I thought. Carol's phone rang and I wondered what to do. Before I could wonder too long she was back in the kitchen, setting down a diaper and some other supplies to pick up the cordless unit in the corner. "Hello. Yes?" There was a long silence from her end and her shoulders under the loose-woven white sweater looked taut. "Look, this isn't a good time. Ollie's ready to go down for his nap and I've got company." She didn't say any more than that, but it felt like she was trying to telegraph something to the person on the other end with her words. For a moment I actually wondered if it could be Edna. There was just something about the way Carol glanced at me quickly, and then looked away that had a touch of guilt to it.

Whoever it was, Carol ended the conversation with very little else to say, and came back to the table, taking the fussy Ollie from me. In a few short moments he was changed, washed up and in a clean one-piece outfit and back in her arms taking a bottle. He twirled the fingers of his left hand through his hair while the right hand grasped the bottle in that sleepy, preoccupied set of gestures that said he would be dropping off soon.

"Look, I don't want to seem like I'm kicking you out, but he'll settle down a lot faster without anybody else here." Since the phone call Carol seemed jumpy. It only deepened my suspicions that Edna had been on the other end of the line.

I could be wrong, I knew. She could just be a tired middle-aged grandmother taking care of an active kid, looking forward to a little time for herself once he went down for that nap. "Can I call you later once I know more about the services?"

"Sure. If I come, it will be for Becca. Like I said before, I've been over Dennis for years. I hope you get over him soon. It's a healthier life, being over Dennis Peete." Tears formed quickly in her eyes and then vanished just as quickly, unshed. "Do you mind letting yourself out?" She nodded down toward Ollie, who'd drifted off still sucking the bottle.

I thanked her for her time and the coffee, and picked up my purse to leave. Retracing my path, I went out through the front room and into the small entrance hall. There was another cordless phone handset on the washstand there, and seeing it made me overwhelmingly tempted to do something shady. I could hear Carol in the kitchen humming to the baby, and silently I picked up the cordless phone and pushed a button. As I'd hoped, the last caller showed up on the display with a name and time. It logged on as five minutes ago, and the caller ID said "Miller, Brandon J."

I put the phone down as quietly as possible and went back out to my car, thinking about everything Carol had said, and what I'd just found out. I had plenty to think about again, and none of the answers I'd hoped to get by talking to Carol. And now I was even surer that she knew exactly where Edna was.

Why else would someone be calling from Becca's when both of Ollie's parents were supposed to be at work and Carol was watching the baby? And how could I explain my suspicions to anybody else without looking awful? The truth was that I was just going to have to 'fess up and look awful, because it was the only way to get around what I more than just suspected now.

If I had known where that condo or apartment was already, I probably would have tried to confront Edna myself. Not the brightest idea in the world, but the best one I had right now. As it was, I didn't have any choice but to go back to Detective Fernandez and tell him. He had Becca's address and was probably the only person who wanted to find Edna more than I did. I'd just have to put up with the fireworks that were bound to occur when I told him the truth about how I'd found the information.

10

Fireworks there were, the moment that Detective Fernandez heard what I had to say. He wasn't exactly appreciative of the fact that I'd looked at somebody else's caller ID, and he didn't like any of my ideas on how he should check things out at this point, either.

I'd chickened out on driving straight to the sheriff's substation from Carol's house, and gone back to Edna's to make a phone call instead. Our first couple of sentences of conversation were pleasant, because the detective was doing all the talking.

"I was getting ready to call you. The medical examiner's office notified me this afternoon that they're releasing Mr. Peete's body to Dodd and Sons. So you're free to go ahead with whatever plans you have."

I thanked him for the information, took a deep breath and told him where I'd been and what I'd done there. The silence on the phone stretched to uncomfortable dimensions, and the only thing that I could hear was what sounded like fingers drumming or some other sound of frustration. I'd seen Fernandez enough times now to picture that look like a forming migraine that went along with the drumming. It started getting more intense when I went ahead and told him about the caller ID and my theory.

"So now you think I should just go over there with lights blazing and sirens on and bust into the Millers' apartment to find out if they're harboring a fugitive?"

It sounded pretty awful when put that way, and totally impractical. "No, of course not. It's just that we've all been looking for Edna, and now we know where she is—"

"Maybe. Nobody knows for sure unless Carol Peete really was talking to her. And that's something I can't very well just call her up and ask, now, can I? Because you just told me that she said she'd had no contact with her former mother-in-law, so you wouldn't have any real, legal reason to think otherwise, would you, Ms. Harris?"

"I guess not. This was all a mistake, wasn't it? I just thought you'd want the information."

His voice was even more strident when he answered. "What information? I haven't heard any information yet, just a few off-track guesses from somebody who shouldn't be nosing around in the first place."

He was probably right. I didn't want to give him the satisfaction of admitting that, but it was difficult not to. For a change I felt really bad about what I'd done. "I suppose I should go back to just planning Dennis's funeral.

I'm assuming that will be Friday now, sometime in the morning. I'll need to call either Carol or Becca with that information, though. Is that all right, Detective?"

There was a long sigh from his end of the phone. "As long as all you do is call either of them, and stick to that topic alone, I don't think we have another problem, Ms. Harris. Am I clear on that?"

"You're clear as crystal. Am I also allowed to talk to someone at the newspaper office to let them know about service plans?"

"Of course. As long as you're discussing your husband's services, you can talk to just about anybody on the planet." The detective sounded very tired. "Now if you don't mind, I need to get back to work."

I said goodbye and hung up, feeling like I'd messed up everything in just one afternoon. Maybe he was right; maybe I should just go about the business of planning Dennis's funeral and let someone else worry about who killed him. I knew that I didn't, and I was pretty sure that Heather hadn't. At the same time I had to admit that conviction was just based on the other things I'd seen of her as a person, and the fact that she might have had a dose of the same GHB that was meant for me.

Besides that, what did I know, really? Carol could have been talking to anybody on the phone. It could even have been Becca herself, sneaking home for a moment alone for a change without the demands of husband, job and baby that she'd taken on awfully young. I'd been in that situation at her age, and it suddenly struck me how much I treasured every free, unencumbered moment, and how far between they'd been. I felt very tired and quite mixed-up.

There were still a few things I needed to do whether I was tired or not, and the most important things all involved what I told Detective Fernandez that I'd do, namely planning Dennis's funeral. First I called Scott Dodd at the mortuary, who assured me that he had been contacted by the county medical examiner's office and everything was under control. He also had the further good news that there apparently was a plan at least partially paid for in Dennis's name, purchased by Edna. Now all we needed to do was find her and get another signature and that would be taken care of. I assured him that as soon as I found her, I'd be sending her over to give him that signature. In my mind, I decided that I'd even get that taken care of before I sent her over to Detective Fernandez when and if she showed up.

A second call to the church office at Conejo Community Chapel let Pastor George in on what was happening. He wasn't in the office himself, but Helen took down everything and I trusted her to get the details to him.

After that it was a toss-up as to which call to make next. I owed one to Sam Blankenship at the *Star,* and I really wanted to talk to my mom. In the end duty won out and I called Sam first. He sounded really excited about hearing from me until I told him that I just wanted to tell him about services and when they'd be held. "I guess I better transfer you over to the obituary desk then," he said, sounding glum.

"No, wait." There was a rattling in the background as if he had a bag of something on the desk. It sounded like a rattling snack bag, maybe microwave popcorn or vending-machine chips. I could imagine either being dinner for a hardworking, broke young reporter. "Let me take down everything about the services. I bet the killer will be there. Maybe something big will happen." I knew he was really just thinking out loud and optimistically as far as he was concerned. I didn't burst his bubble with what I thought about his notions, just told him that things were set up for Friday morning at eleven at Dodd and Sons in Rancho Conejo and left it at that. Then he transferred me over to the obituary desk, as he put it, and I gave them all of the information a second time. I hoped that if the information ran in the newspaper for a day or two, perhaps it would jolt Edna out of hiding.

Thinking about that jolted me into making one more call, to Carol's house. She didn't pick up the phone, and I was forced to leave a message about the services for Dennis. I thought I'd call her back later and make sure I talked to her in person. I wanted to make sure Becca got the information, and that she participated as much as she chose to in her father's funeral. She and I hadn't exactly gotten along so far and I owed that much to her.

All the duty calls finally done, I made a pot of herbal tea, having decided that I'd caffeinated myself enough for the next two days already, and got ready to call my mom and my son. Taking my teacup and a phone into the living room, I noticed all sorts of windows open on my computer screen. Ben had sent me about half a dozen instant messages since he'd gotten home from school.

I made a mental note to change my settings on the computer so that somebody sending me an IM would make some noise. I'd set everything to silent several weeks ago when I'd gotten tired of Edna clucking in dismay every time a chime sounded on the computer. She was sure, no matter how many times I told her otherwise, that long-distance communication like that *had* to cost something. In her opinion I was being incredibly wasteful with money to be that free with it, just instant messaging all over the place. In the long run it was easier to take the noises away. She wasn't computer literate enough to know that I was still doing all that annoying instant messaging without the noise.

Really, she hadn't liked computer noises in general, which is why I'd taken to setting almost everything on every program so that it didn't activate any noises, or wore headphones most of the time. Of course, that was a problem, as well, given that I startle very easily. I'd be sitting at the screen, typing away on something for school, IM-ing with Ben while I listened to a CD with headphones on, and Edna would come up behind me and tap me on the shoulder. That was all it took for me to shriek like a banshee and rise straight out of my chair. And then conflict would start all over again.

In that respect it was so much more peaceful without her here. Still, I would have welcomed a little noise and conflict if I'd known she was okay. Having her gone this long was just too weird. Sighing about it all, I put the phone down along with my cup of tea and tried to get hold of my plugged-in offspring. He had an "away" message up, saying something cryptic that I suspected would only make sense if one was another seventeen-year-old, but I sent him a brief "Hi, it's Mom" instant message anyway.

In thirty seconds he'd replied and we were typing away to each other. School was okay, he maintained, even though it sounded more with each passing week like he was courting senioritis to me. He hadn't heard from any of his college choices yet, but hoped to soon.

He had come out to California for Thanksgiving and we'd looked at a few schools here, including Pacific Oaks. He'd applied there and to a couple other California institutions of higher learning, as well as to the Missouri state schools where most of his classmates were going. Even though I had no idea how we were going to pay for it, I still hoped he'd get in one of the schools he had applied to out my way so that we could be under the same roof part of the time.

There was still the possibility that I could just move back to Missouri and start over. Tonight, as I sat alone in Edna's darkening living room, it didn't sound as bad an idea as it once had. Still, if I did that, my chances of getting the money Dennis had made disappear were as gone as the money. "Is GMa around?" I asked Ben in shorthand on the computer.

"Nope. Bird-watchers or some club or something," he shot back. "I've got music on double loud while I do homework and study for my physics test."

Since the one luxury I'd insisted on paying for when I gave my mother money for Ben's care and feeding was a high-speed DSL modem for each of us, I was still free to call him and talk for real at the same time even though my mom wasn't there to talk to, just my adorable offspring. It was easier on me than the constant typing, although that was Ben's favored mode of communication. "Turn it down a little, because I'm about to call you."

There was a long pause and then a one-word message back. "Rats."

I punched in the phone number, and he picked up on the first ring. "Benjamin Mitchell Harris, are you gaming while you're doing your homework and listening to music?"

"Hello to you, too, Mom. So nice of you to call. And of course I'm doing no such thing," he replied smoothly.

Of course he probably *was* instant messaging with eight different kids at once, most of them girls besides his best buddy, Dave. "Hi, son. And I'm glad to hear you're keeping to the straight and narrow. Somebody's got to be."

"Hey, you sound tired. Everything okay? Or as okay as it's going to be?" He sounded so mature when he got concerned about me that it made my throat constrict.

"The second one. It's about as okay as it's going to get anytime soon. We finally got the okay to set service times for Dennis." I didn't say "your stepfather" because that was one area where Dennis had been more lacking than any other. He and Ben hadn't ever really bonded.

"Mom-zilla ever show back up?" I winced at his nickname for Edna. They'd been less than bosom buddies when he'd come out for Thanksgiving. Apparently her opinion of any teenager compared to her own darling Dennis in years past was low, and she'd made it quite obvious what she thought of my baby.

"Not yet. I'm actually getting really worried about her."

"Wow, you must be taking this going-back-to-church thing seriously." I'd told him about the Christian Friends and the chapel, but hadn't been sure until now whether he'd really heard me or not. "I mean, if you're being that kind to your enemies and all."

"She's hardly an enemy, Ben. For the most part she's a lonely, worried old lady. And now I'm worried about her."

"Maybe you shouldn't be. Maybe she just couldn't handle all of this and lit out for Mexico or something. You said you were what, three hours from Tijuana, right?"

The image of Edna "lighting out for Mexico" almost made me snort herbal tea out my nose. If anybody I knew was incapable of that kind of flight, it was Edna Peete. "On a good day, we're three hours from Tijuana. On a bad day we're three hours from LAX. And I don't expect she headed toward either."

"If you say so. Hey, Mom?"

He even paused to turn his music down a little more, which I thought was helpful of the kid. I could hear clicking in the background, which meant he was still active at the keyboard while we talked. That was okay. He was seventeen. He could multitask.

"Yes, Ben?"

"Do you want me to come out for Friday? I could. Grandma would even come if I talked her into it, I know." Now my throat constricted even more. He had never cared for Dennis, but would come out here to support me if needed. And he was even offering to talk my mother into coming, when it was the world's biggest toss-up as to what she loathed more, Dennis or flying.

"That is so sweet. But no. You stay there and study. Didn't you just tell me that you had a physics test?"

"Well, yeah. But I could get it postponed." I noticed that he didn't say he could take it a day early. That much

Ben wasn't offering to do. He was still the same old Ben and it made me grin.

"No need. Save the trip for another time when I might even need you worse. Besides, it would cost a ton of money if you tried to come out this week. You've still got the sheriff's department number if you get worried, right?"

"Right. It's next to the computer," he said.

"And you've got a name attached to it?" I pushed.

"Yeah. Detective Ray Fernandez. Just like you told me. Honest, I have it all."

"Good. Hopefully you won't ever need it. For now we can talk like this some times, and IM a lot. That seems to be your favorite form of communication." It was the one thing he'd had in common with Dennis, and I mentioned it.

"You know why that is," he said, while I could hear the different sounds from his computer in the background.

"It's fast?"

There was more clicking and chimes. "Well, that, too. But really, it's because it's so easy. And it happens in real time. And it doesn't leave a trace."

"What do you mean?"

There was one of those sighs teens give their clueless parents. "Mom, IMs don't leave a record. Unless somebody sets things up to put them on digest or records them intentionally, there's no trace once you close the window you're in or sign off. And almost nobody ever does digest."

"Oh." Now I knew why Dennis preferred them. And here I'd felt so racy and trendy and "fun" instant messaging with him. Meanwhile he was just covering his tracks as usual. The house felt even colder and darker than it had a moment before. Even my tea had cooled off.

We talked a few minutes more, and before I hung up I made it a point to tell my son how much I loved him. Wonder of wonders, the almost impossible happened. Before Ben put down his phone he said the magic words out loud. "I love you, too, Mom. Good night." After he hung up I went all around the house turning on lights. Edna would have kittens if she came home right now, but tonight I needed to battle the darkness in clear and obvious ways.

I went to sleep that night with most of those lights burning. It was nice to wake up to them in the morning, even if I felt terribly wasteful. I guess I'd almost hoped that somehow having the lights on all night would perversely draw Edna home to cluck at my spendthrift ways. But I was still just as alone in the house when I woke up as when I'd gone to sleep.

I'd taken to checking her bedroom the first thing every morning. Given our spectacular lack of communication in the past, there was more than a slim chance that Edna, when she came home, would just slip on into her bedroom without so much as a "Hi, honey, I'm home." Not that she'd ever call me "honey" in real life. I was still more than half convinced that the first real hint I'd get that Edna was back would be a load of laundry running, not a hearty hello.

I made a halfhearted effort to look at my schoolbooks in the morning while I toyed with coffee and toast. Soon I was either going to have to buckle down and go back to class and work hard or drop the semester. Most of my classes had had four or five meetings by now, and I'd been to the first one and no more. As Heather had predicted, the instructors were sympathetic when I'd e-mailed or called them with my predicament, but they wouldn't be sympathetic forever. Paging through the books didn't give me an answer right away, so I got busy doing other things.

Another short visit with Scott at Dodd and Sons got everything planned for Friday morning from his end of the preparations. When he'd found the prepaid plan, it included cremation. Dennis's plan didn't come with a specific urn or box for his ashes, so I had the slightly odd task of picking that out. Scott told me that most families brought in a picture, or several, of the deceased to display near the front of the room.

For a moment I got this memory flashback to my first Christian Friends meeting, and wondered if Heather and I should both bring our photos. It would provide a clearer picture of just who Dennis had been. Putting that thought away, I went back to planning.

After Scott had asked a few questions about details, it became clear that we wouldn't need extra time for friends and family to gather on the evening before the services. There weren't that many people I expected to show up to begin with, and what some of us would say to each other for more than fifteen minutes, I hadn't a clue. So we settled on having the chapel open an hour before the 11:00 a.m. services, and left it at that.

It would feel odd not having the night before what old-timers in Missouri at least would have called a wake. I didn't know enough about funeral customs here to know if such a thing was ever done, even for those who had enough family and friends to warrant it. I decided to ask Linnette if the offers of help that she'd given me through Christian Friends would include something more informal. Maybe the group could come by the house Thursday night.

As soon as I thought that, I realized I'd have to work fast if I wanted anything like that to happen. Thursday was *tomorrow*. The only plus to time moving as fast as it seemed to be was that soon this whole experience would be over and I could pick up the pieces of what was going to be my normal life from now on. I was beginning to feel anxious to see what "normal" was going to be. After the past few weeks, normal would be interesting.

Fortunately Linnette was quite accommodating. "Sure, we can do that. I'd pretty much figured we would if you wanted to. Any chance that Dennis's daughter and her mom will join us?"

"I can ask them. I need to call and let them know about all the other plans. But I kind of doubt they're going to want to do anything social with me, especially if Heather is involved, as well."

"Hey, God works in some strange ways in folks' hearts sometimes," Linnette said, sounding far more chipper than I could be today. "Plant the seed, anyway. It could happen."

"I'll do that."

"And plan on us bringing all of the food. I have a feeling you never did go out and do a lot of grocery shopping and organize menus like we discussed, did you?"

"Not exactly." I wasn't about to tell her that dinner last night had been a frozen entrée I'd had to chip out of a freezer compartment in the garage. No use in upsetting somebody who was being this wonderful.

"Okay. I'll call everybody else besides Heather, and the rest of Dennis's family. See you tomorrow night a little before seven, all right?"

"Sounds good." It sounded so much more than good. It sounded like having a home and a family again, something that had been sorely lacking in the past few weeks. And it even gave me the strength to call Heather and then Carol.

Heather was enthusiastic about coming. As I'd predicted, Carol wasn't. She sounded like she couldn't believe that somebody wanted to celebrate anything connected with her ex-husband's life or death. She did promise to tell Becca all about it, but warned me that her daughter was working late that evening so she probably wouldn't attend.

"What about Friday morning?" I almost held my breath waiting for her to answer. "Do you think Becca will want to say anything if we ask for remembrances from people?" If anybody had something kind to say about Dennis, it would have been either his daughter or his mother. At this point I was losing hope that his mother would even show up to attend the services.

There was quite a pause on the other end. "I can't imagine it. Besides, Becca wants to bring Ollie so that I can come, too, and I don't think Brandon's going to be able to get off work on such short notice. So she won't want to get up with a baby in her arms."

"All right." It was almost a relief to hear that. I'd rather think about the baby's presence at the services than wonder what kind of loose-cannon remarks Becca might make. "I'll see you then, I guess."

"Looks like it." She said goodbye and hung up without any more discussion. So there I was ready for another thrilling afternoon at the old homestead. Maybe, I thought, it was time to go back to class just to get my mind off of some of the rest of this. If I hurried I could catch the afternoon lecture section in my "Theories of Educational Psychology" class. Even that beat hanging around Edna's living room staring at the walls. And if I timed things right, I could grab a latte with Linnette before she headed home.

11

On Thursday I actually went to both of my classes. It beat sitting in the house thinking about everything that was happening. Going to campus convinced me that if I worked hard at this, I didn't have to worry about dropping my courses this semester. In the long run, the quicker that I got my act together and got my degree, the faster I'd be able to really support myself and Ben when he started college in the fall, wherever that would be.

Between classes I even went in to the Coffee Corner and talked to Maria. I think she would have hired me on the spot if I'd been available, but she was willing to give me another week to get my life together. We went over the various forms I would need, and she told me where to take copies to the graduate office so that my hours as a barista would be registered under work study. When I went over to tell Linnette about my success, she beamed.

"This is the kind of thing you need right now. You'll have to tell everybody tonight. They'll be happy for you."

"I'll make a point of it. Remind me if I forget, will you?"

"Definitely. See you before seven. I'll be the one with the pan of lasagna." Even if it was the frozen stuff from the warehouse store, I couldn't begin to tell her how good that sounded. Just a homey meal with other people sounded like a grand idea.

When I came into the house that afternoon I somehow saw it with a stranger's eyes when I walked through the door. It needed some work. So instead of studying for a couple hours I did all the things that Edna would have been doing all week, had she been here. All the newspapers I'd piled in the kitchen got recycled, the trash got dumped and I did a quick damp mop of the kitchen floor.

After that there was vacuuming, a little bit of dusting and even throwing in a couple of loads of laundry. It was amazing how much difference those few things made in the way the house looked, and in my attitude. Suddenly I was ready to think about the future again. It was almost as if I'd been drifting for a couple weeks since I'd met up with Linnette and gone to that first Christian Friends meeting. Now, I had a purpose, even if tonight that purpose was only to get through the next two days. After that I could move on from there when the time came.

I had time for a quick shower and even got a little bit of reading done on my psychology class assignments before the doorbell rang the first time at six forty-five. As promised, Linnette was there, and she had a sturdy nine-by-thirteen pan with her.

"Homemade lasagna? You really are my new best friend," I told her, ushering her into the house.

"Hey, for most occasions the store-bought stuff does just fine, but this bunch is picky and I figured we needed the best we could get tonight."

I had to agree with her. We put the oven on low and tucked in her meal, and stood in the kitchen getting plates and silver out while we waited for the others to show up. In the next twenty minutes they all came in. Dot had a big salad and a loaf of wonderful-smelling garlic bread with her, Heather came bearing several two-liter containers of soft drinks and Lexy brought brownies.

By about a quarter after seven we were all in Edna's dining room, having the nicest gathering I'd ever been part of in that room. There hadn't been too many events in that room in the time I'd lived here. Dennis was on the road too much when he was healthy, and Edna had given up any socializing once he'd had his accident. Other than the very tense Thanksgiving dinner that she and Ben and I had shared, I didn't have much to compare this to.

Everybody passed food around, talking softly and visiting with their neighbors. We all fit well there, and even the others that we'd hoped to have had there would have fit pretty well. I wasn't surprised that Carol had passed on the gathering, but was a little sad that Becca hadn't chosen to join us. I still wanted to see if I couldn't get to know her in a friendly kind of way. Maybe it just wasn't ever going to happen.

The oddest missing person was Edna, any way you wanted to describe it. It was odd that she was still missing, and even when she turned up she'd probably be a bit odd. I had even less hope of ever knowing where she'd been for certain in the past ten days than I had of making friends with Becca. All these thoughts were still swirling around in my head when Linnette got us to pay attention long enough to say grace over dinner.

"Lord, thank You for bringing us together to support each other as we mourn the untimely passing of Dennis Peete and remember his life at the same time. Help Gracie Lee to find comfort. Help Heather to find peace. Thank You for leading both of them into our group of Christian Friends to enrich us all. Thank You for this time to be together, and for this food to nourish our bodies as we do Your work. In Jesus' name we pray."

Everybody gave a firm "Amen" and the next few minutes were filled with the busy work of dinner, passing grated cheese and salt and pepper, making sure everybody had a napkin, and the little things that I'd almost forgotten were part of a meal for a group of people. It felt like ages since I'd eaten with friendly folks.

Maybe that was what made the tears start. Or maybe it was just everything hitting me at once. All I knew was that one moment I thought I was fine, and the next my eyes were burning and my throat was tight. I added very little to the conversation at the table, mostly listening while the others talked about church stuff.

Paula, we found out, was closing on a house deal tonight and so couldn't have joined us. Her absence didn't seem to be felt too badly by anybody. "How long has she been part of the group?" What I really wanted to ask was why she was there, since she seemed to be so tightly held together that I couldn't imagine why she came.

"I guess about three years now. She comes and goes as she feels the need," Linnette said.

Dot nodded. "Most of the time she's stopped coming, but this time of year is hard for her, so she comes back for a while." She looked over at Linnette. "Can I say more, as long as it's something that anybody in the church or the community would know?"

Linnette nodded. "We're not that confidential, just for stuff that only the group holds in common."

Dot went on then. "Three years ago, Paula's daughter was in a car with four other teenagers out for a ride. It was late at night and rainy and the driver hadn't had his license for long. He wasn't really legal yet to have other kids in the car with him, but he did, anyway."

I didn't like where this was going. The last thing I wanted was to feel sympathy for Paula. That probably made me a very bad person, but it was how I felt right now. It was so much easier to keep my image of her as mean, snarky and uptight instead of a hurt, grieving mother. Dot wasn't letting me rest, though. "The police said that the driver of the SUV that hit them had a blood alcohol level that should have made him unconscious. Of course, *he* lived through the accident. Nobody in the car that Ashley was in did. Four of them, including Ashley, died at the scene. One of the girls in the back seat lived about a week."

It was hard to imagine what Paula must have gone through. Maybe she'd been a perfectly happy, friendly person before her daughter's death. I decided then and there I'd try and make the effort the next time I saw her to be more pleasant. It couldn't hurt anything.

"Now *my* mother, on the other hand, was just as unpleasant before I came home single and pregnant as she is now," Heather said, one side of her mouth quirking up in a wry grin. She looked around the table. "Well, it's true and you would all probably admit it. I don't think I've done anything to please her since the fourth grade talent show when I lost a tap off my shoe."

"Moms usually want what's best for their kids, or at least what they think is best," Linnette said, defusing some of the tension a little. "It's too bad that those aren't always the same thing."

"You're telling me," Heather said. "I'm really beginning to wonder whether I want to stay there once the baby's born."

"Your mother will probably adore having a grandbaby," Dot said. "I know that I would. If you're serious about looking for a place, I could offer you one, though." Dot looked across the table at me. "That goes for either of you, actually."

"Does this mean you're ready to rent out the carriage house again?" Lexy asked her.

Dot chuckled. "That's a very kind description, Alexis. I'd hardly call the apartment over our garage a carriage house."

Lexy shook her head. "It's way nicer than she's told you, Gracie Lee. She and Buck built this apartment for Candace and a friend, as sort of a transition."

"And eventually she transitioned out of it. It's sat empty most of the time for about four years," Dot explained. "It really needs some renovation, but if you could put up with that, there's a place that would be big enough for either of you alone, or even the two of you if you needed it and that didn't seem too…odd," she finished.

"I'll think about it. I need someplace else, and will have to move on soon. Even if Dennis's mom walked in the door this evening, I can't imagine we'd get along well together without him here." It was the first time I'd admitted that out loud to somebody else. I'd thought it before, but never said it. The admission felt good. Maybe our differences were mostly my fault, but they were real. And admitting the problem out loud made the reality a solid thing.

"You were never meant to," Linnette said. "He was the glue that held your relationship—such as it was—together."

"And now he's gone." That was the first time I'd said that out loud, too, and I wasn't prepared for the effect it had on me. He really was gone, wasn't he? "Wow. Maybe I've just realized what that really means. He's not coming back."

Heather was nodding, and her eyes were full, but not running over. I could feel the tears on my own cheeks, and for a change I didn't care. "When he was in the care center, there was at least a chance that he would come back someday. That I'd get a chance to tell him how angry I was with him, and how much I loved him at the same time."

"It bothered me for months that the last thing I said to him was 'Fine. Why don't you just leave, then?' and he did," Heather said, sounding on the verge of a sob. "But once I'd seen him in that bed, I knew it wasn't because of me that he'd left. It was his fault, too.

"When I saw him, I remembered the last thing he'd said to me. I'd told him I was pregnant, and he'd had the nerve to ask if it was his. 'Of course it is,' I'd said, 'because there hasn't ever been anybody else.' Then he started yelling, asking me how I could be that stupid, and why did he stay? That's when I told him to leave."

Oh, Dennis. I wondered if there had ever been a woman in his life he hadn't first charmed then wounded to the core, and used in the process. And at the same time here we were crying over him now that he was dead, and if Carol had been here, she would have been doing the same thing. It didn't make any sense, yet here we were.

I was crying harder now and somebody was rubbing my shoulder. It was probably Linnette, but I didn't even look up. "What am I going to do?" I asked the room in general. "I've got no money, a kid to support who is ready to go to college, no job to speak of, nothing. I'm living in a house I probably have no right to be in, and Dennis cheated me out of thirty thousand dollars and then died. What on earth am I going to do?"

There was silence for a while, and a little sniffling joining mine. Then Dot stood up from her place across the table from me and came over to pat the shoulder that Linnette wasn't rubbing. "I was waiting for you to ask that. You're going to survive, sweetie. It's what women have been doing since Eve. You're going to survive, with God's help and guidance, and we're all here to get you through it."

Knowing at that moment that everybody in this room had been as down as I was now, at least once, should have helped. It really should have. But it didn't right away, and so those wonderful women surrounding me just let me bawl like a baby for a good solid half hour before they told me to settle down and broke out the brownies.

"You are not staying here alone tonight," Heather was the one to say firmly about nine-thirty when things began to wind down.

For once I couldn't argue with her. I had no desire to spend tonight alone in this house. "You're right, but I can't leave. There's still the off chance that Edna could come home, and I don't want to be gone if she does." Of course it was the slimmest of chances, but it was still possible, so I hung on to it.

"I know. I figured you'd say that, and I kind of thought something like this might happen," she said, gesturing at the crumpled tissues littering the table and floor around me. "So I packed an overnight bag."

It sounded wonderful to have her company, but I felt a stab of guilt at the same time. "I hate to ask you to do this."

"Lexy and Dot have somebody waiting for them at home. My mom didn't exactly sound unhappy to have me gone for the night. I think she misses the peace and quiet she's used to." Heather sounded wistful and I wondered if it was because her mom didn't necessarily want her there, or if she missed her own peace and quiet back in the apartment she'd lived in before.

Linnette made a wry face. "I'd offer to stay with you two, but I have to get up about five and go into the bookstore. If I'm going to duck out at ten for the funeral, I have to go in early and make sure that everything's ready to start inventory."

"You're a good friend. You put all this together, and

now you're getting up before it's even light just to help me out again tomorrow. We'll be fine," I told her, looking around in awe at the wonderful bunch of women God had sent me. It was very clear by now that God had sent them to me, or me to them, however we wanted to put it. "Go home and get into bed before you have to get back up again."

Linnette wrinkled her nose. "I will. But I first want to make sure you two are okay." She looked thoughtful for a minute. "Are you going to get any sleep at all?"

I shrugged. "I can try, anyway. Maybe with having somebody else here it will be easier."

"Didn't the doctor ever give you anything in all these months to settle your nerves or help you sleep?" Dot asked. "It seems like that's the first thing they do nowadays."

"Now that you mention it, I do have something." There had been a doctor at the Board and Care who had been very concerned about me, as well as Dennis, in his first days there. When she'd questioned me about whether I was eating and sleeping, I'd admitted I wasn't doing much of either, and she'd written me a prescription and nagged me into filling it. I'd taken three or four nights' worth of the tablets, then gotten into a better routine and they'd sat unused in the medicine cabinet.

"Since you have company tonight, it might be the time to take something, then," Linnette said. "Tomorrow's going to be rough, and it would help if you got a good night's sleep."

"You're right. Once you all head off I'll get into my jammies and take what the doctor ordered."

"Good. See that she actually does it, will you?" Linnette said to Heather, back to being her organized self. "I'll see you about ten-fifteen tomorrow morning at Dodd and Sons, then." She gathered up her stuff, as did everybody but Heather, and they made their goodbyes and left. It had been good to have them here, and almost as good for them to head home and let things wind down.

Heather looked almost as tired as I felt. "How about we see what the clean sheet situation is in the guest room, and call it a night?" I asked her. "We can always deal with whatever else there is to do in the kitchen when we get up in the morning."

"Works for me. Just don't forget that sleeping pill, Gracie Lee, or Linnette will be on my case for days."

"I won't forget." I really thought that as worn out as I was, I could probably do without it, but if I did that, I'd be staring at the ceiling about 3:00 a.m. So I went around the main part of the house with Heather, checking doors to make sure they were locked and lights were turned off, just like my regular routine. It was nice to have someone else to do it with me.

The guest room, which was really Edna's sewing room with a twin bed tucked in a corner, had clean sheets on the bed, but presented a little problem when I looked at it and compared the width of that twin bed with Heather's midsection. It was hard to imagine somebody close to her ninth month of pregnancy getting comfortable in that bed.

"Tell you what," I told her. "How about we put clean sheets on the queen bed in my room and you take that one?"

"I can't take your bed," she said halfheartedly, looking at that narrow one with its soft mattress.

"Sure you can. I'd even rather you did tonight. To tell the truth, after all the revelations earlier, I'm not looking forward to being in there alone. Switching this way will benefit both of us. You'll get enough room to toss and turn, and I can be someplace that doesn't remind me of Dennis tonight."

She smiled. "Once you put it that way, I don't feel bad about taking your bed. Let's get it made up so we can both go to sleep. For a change I'm plenty ready."

"Not sleeping well?"

"Just fitfully. I've started getting up to go to the bathroom or walk off leg cramps once or twice most nights. Guess that's to get me ready to get up two or three times a night soon, huh?"

"Hey, maybe you'll get lucky. Maybe your baby will be the one who sleeps through the night at three or four weeks."

Her eyes widened. "Does that really happen?"

"I've heard it said. Not by me, but I've heard it said. You could ask the rest of the group at Christian Friends sometime."

I headed toward the linen closet in the hall and got the clean sheets for my bed. With two of us working, the bed was made in no time, and we were each in one of the bathrooms getting ready for bed. Once Heather came out of the hall bath I ducked in there long enough to grab a sleeping pill. Even with taking one, I suspected that it would be difficult to get to sleep in the narrow, lumpy guest room bed.

I suspected wrong. I didn't even get all my evening prayers said, given everybody I wanted to bless, before I drifted off. It wasn't a deep sleep, but the medication pulled me under to a point where even when I heard something moving around deep in the night, I didn't get up.

Instead, I remembered Heather saying that she was up frequently, and said a quick prayer for her leg cramps or whatever was keeping her from sleeping as soundly as I was, and drifted back off. When I woke up the next time it was morning, or at least almost morning. It wasn't quite full daylight yet, but the sky outside the thin curtains in the guest room was lightening up. Like most February mornings, the heat had kicked on and I could hear the growling hum of the blower pushing warm air through the house.

The furnace seemed louder than usual, or deeper or something. And as I began to sit up I noticed that my head ached and I felt like I was coming down with something. *Great. Of all days, why today?* The last thing I needed today was some kind of virus. Maybe it was just all the crying last night. I didn't usually do anything like that, and it could have been that kind of trauma that made me feel queasy and slow this morning.

I really hoped it wasn't catching, whatever was making me feel like this. I felt bad waking up this morning, but I'd feel even worse if I'd given all the Christian Friends some kind of nasty virus and they had to come to Dennis's funeral feeling like I felt now. At this point the prospect of going myself didn't sound too great.

I sat on the edge of the bed trying to figure out what would help the most. A cold drink was what I needed first to ease this scratchy throat, if I could keep anything down. I got up and caught myself against the chair Edna kept next to her sewing machine. Why was I staggering?

I thought I'd remembered closing the door when I went to bed, but it was open now. Going out into the hall, everything looked blurry or funny. And it smelled even worse. I had no idea what was going on, but it wasn't good. This had to be the worst virus or whatever I'd had in a long time. Maybe taking the sleeping pill had been a very bad idea. I'd slept deeply, but waking up feeling this putrid wasn't worth it.

When I switched the bathroom light on I was shocked by how awful I looked to go along with the awful way I felt. My face was flushed and blotchy, what I could see of it. There was a blur about everything, and my hands were shaking as I tried to get the water glass under the tap to get a drink. Along with the aching there were alarms going off in my brain now, telling me that something was wrong, something more serious than just a twenty-four-hour bug.

I left the glass of water on the bathroom countertop and went back out into the hall. The humming noise I heard was much louder than just the furnace running, and it seemed to be coming from the laundry room. Stumbling in the dark, I fumbled for the light switch in the narrow space. When I reached it, I stood there blinking. The door to the garage was open, and the noise was coming from there.

Edna's blue car was in its usual spot. That should have made me very happy under normal circumstances. Standing in the doorway, the source of the noise finally dawned on me. Not only was Edna's car there, it was still running in the closed garage, and probably had been for some time. And the door to the house had been left open.

I was coughing now, about to choke. My responses were so slow. I knew I should do something about all this, because a running car in a closed space wasn't good. Reaching out my left hand, I hit the garage door opener mounted on the wall and the door swung slowly open, letting cool, blessed fresh air into the garage.

With the extra light, I could see that there was someone sitting in the driver's seat of the car. My balance was still off, and I lurched more than ran over to the driver's side of the car. The window was open and I reached in, turning off the ignition. "Edna?" Calling her came out as a croak. It was her in the front seat, but she wasn't moving. I shook her shoulder and she slumped toward the other side of the car. I couldn't see or feel her breathing, and one more thing finally got into my foggy brain. Heather was still inside the house.

Reeling away from the car, I went back inside. The door to my bedroom was open, too, and Heather was half on the bed, half on the floor, as if she'd tried to get out of bed but lost the effort. "Come on, we have to get you out of here," I said, trying to get her roused enough to help me walk her outside.

Partly dragging her, partly coaxing her up to walk, we headed to the patio at the back of the house, as far from the garage as I could get. The cool, fresh air seemed to revive her a little and I left Heather in a chair, coughing and threatening to throw up.

Going back into the house for as little time as possible I grabbed a phone and called 911. Somehow I had the presence of mind to tell the person I reached on the other end of the line that we needed the sheriff's department, as well as the fire and ambulance service. I even thought to mention Ray's name.

Then, even though it was the last thing I wanted to do, I went back to the garage to wait for the sirens and trucks, and to keep Edna company one last time.

12

The paramedics—two men and a woman—came first, rolling up in an ambulance. I pointed them toward Edna and in a few short moments they confirmed quickly what I already knew. Pulling her out of the car, they went through the motions, but it didn't take long for them to give up on trying to get her breathing again. Once I saw that, I started shaking harder than I had been before.

Edna had been gone for a while, and she'd nearly taken Heather and me with her. I'd always expected her to come home eventually, but certainly not like this. Once they'd ascertained that they couldn't do anything for her, they turned their attention to me. "Were you inside that house?" the taller of the two men asked. He looked like a surfer dude grown up a little, dark tan, streaked blond hair and broad shoulders in his navy blue uniform. The

crow's feet around his eyes could have been from squint-
ing into the sun or from his actual age.

I nodded. "The door between the garage and the house
was open, too. And I have no idea how long the car was
in this closed garage." It hurt a little to talk, and I was
afraid I was going to start coughing again, or throwing up.

"If we get the stretcher out, can we get you to lay
down on it while somebody takes your vitals?" the guy
asked. I noticed that the writing above the pocket of his
uniform shirt said Steve.

"If there's only one stretcher, there's somebody who
needs it more," I said, and he cut me off.

"I'm afraid not, ma'am. She's…uh…not going to need
the stretcher. Was she your mother?"

I shook my head, which was a mistake. The movement
made my whole head throb, and the pain got me even
more nauseated. It really made me want to find someplace to sit down, and fast. "No. My mother-in-law, but
we can talk about her later. I had a friend staying the
night. She's on the back patio, and she's not feeling well.
And she's pregnant. Her name is Heather," I called out
as the other two rushed around the corner of the house.

They were still in the backyard and I was still arguing
with Steve a few minutes later about whether or not I was
going to the hospital, when Ray Fernandez showed up.
He and Steve went nose to nose for a while in a heated
discussion about crime scene damage versus taking care
of live people and those originally thought to be alive.
While they were still making their individual points very
loudly, the other two paramedics came around the corner of the house with the gurney, or whatever you called

the stretcher on wheels they were pushing between them. Heather, looking flushed and blotchy under an oxygen mask, was strapped into it.

"Is she okay?" the detective asked, taking his attention off Steve for a moment.

"I think so," the female paramedic said, giving him a telegraphed message with her eyes that said even to me, as a stranger, that she wasn't going to say anything else in front of Heather. Whether or not she was okay, Heather was definitely conscious and able to hear.

Fernandez looked back at Steve. "Look, I know you had to do what you had to do for the people who were still alive. But I'll need a full statement from you and the rest of the crew once you're done transporting the first patient to the hospital. And I'll need prints, just to rule yours out on all the surfaces we'll have to print. Do you think Ms. Harris here is in okay shape to give me a statement first and go to the hospital second?"

I started to protest that I wasn't going to the hospital at all, but the detective wasn't taking any arguments. He was paying attention only to Steve now, who admitted that I would probably be all right long enough to stay here and give him a statement. Unfortunately he also told the detective that I was eventually going to the hospital. At this point I didn't really have the strength to argue with him.

Steve gave an assessing look into the laundry room. "And don't let her go back inside the house and stay there for any length of time until it's aired out for a while, at least half an hour. Longer would be better."

"Can I go in long enough to get a robe and slippers?" I asked.

"Sure. But have him follow you around so if you get woozy again, he can catch you. And only stay long enough to get that stuff, and open a couple windows," Steve instructed. Then he turned his attention to the ambulance, where the other two were loading Heather into the back, the oxygen mask still on her face. In a moment, they were gone.

I went into the house, the detective trailing me at a close distance. He followed me into my bedroom, where my slippers were in a corner. I slid them on my feet, only now aware of the awful old flannel pajamas I'd been wearing. I didn't have to worry about modesty in them, as they had long pants and long sleeves, and fortunately still had all their buttons. The fabric was worn, but there weren't any holes anyplace. They'd faded from their original bright red plaid to paler shades resembling cold tomato soup and concrete gray, and were probably the rattiest thing I owned besides the robe I was about to put on over them, an old blue number I'd been wearing since before Ben was born. It had great sentimental value, was warm and looked hideous.

Suddenly I felt the overwhelming need to comb my hair, among other things. When the detective kept following me as I left the room, I stopped him in the hallway. "You're not going where I end up next. And I promise you can look inside first to prove the window isn't large enough for me to escape, even if I open it all the way. How about you open the windows in the rest of the house, and I'll meet you back here in two minutes?"

"Only two minutes," he said, looking solemn. "And I have a second hand on my watch."

* * *

Ten minutes later we were sitting out on the patio where Heather had been while I called 911. "You could have died in there," Fernandez pointed out, still looking as solemn as he had most of the morning. Once he'd opened all the windows in the house, he'd made me come sit here on the patio with a glass of water, and excused himself to go close the garage and put a note on it for the crime scene technicians to meet him in the back of the house.

"I know that. And I'm even more worried about Heather, because I'm the one who talked her into staying the night with me. If she or the baby is hurt by this—" My throat tightened and I had to stop talking while I coughed.

"I shouldn't push you. We can do this statement later. How about I call another ambulance now?" Fernandez looked more worried than I'd seen him so far, which was saying something.

"I'll be okay. Let's just get this over with. And I have to make a couple phone calls." The worst notification couldn't be made by phone, and I hoped I'd have no part of it. "Will you be talking to Becca and her mother? Becca would be Edna's next of kin now."

"Yeah, that will be my job. And I'll need to do it pretty quickly, which is going to be a problem working this crime scene at the same time. I may call first just to tell them that the funeral won't be happening this morning due to an emergency, so they don't start the drive up here from the Valley."

I hadn't really thought through the logistics of what this was going to do to the funeral arrangements today.

Guess that showed how little of my brain was functioning right now. "Wow. Scott Dodd is going to think this is the most dysfunctional family on the planet."

"He's seen as bad, I'm sure. In any case, it's not unusual for one death to follow another, even though this isn't the way it usually happens. And if he gives you any trouble about postponing the funeral, tell him that official sheriff's department business intervened and give him to me."

It was a kindness he didn't have to show me and I was touched. "What time is it?" I didn't have any clue, other than to know it was fully light now, which meant it was after seven.

Ray looked at his watch. "Seven-thirty. That means you have enough time to tell me about what happened, and make those few calls you need to make before we take you to the hospital. Why don't we start with you telling me what you noticed, and when?"

First I explained briefly why Heather was staying the night. Then I had to tell him straight off that my reactions had been dulled by the sleeping pill. The detective winced a little, but didn't seem totally phased by my admission. As I ran through events in my mind, one thing came back to me. "I heard someone moving around the house last night. It had to be some time after two, but before it got light. At the time I thought it was Heather, because she said she got leg cramps and to expect her up at night."

"But it could have been your mother-in-law?"

"It could have. And one other thing. I was sure that I had closed my bedroom door last night where I slept, in the guest room, but when I got up this morning it was open."

Now he looked grim. "Letting as much fumes as possible into the room." His statement made me shudder again. "What else did you notice when you got up?"

"Mostly how bad I felt. I figured it was the flu or something at first, then I looked in the bathroom mirror and everything seemed off. And there was the noise coming from the garage."

"So the car was still running?"

Nodding to answer him made my head ache worse. I was going to have to stop doing that. "Ouch. Yes. I turned it off by reaching in the window, so my prints will be on the key and the ignition."

"Where else are we likely to find them?" He was writing in his notebook now as he listened.

"On the door leading from the laundry room to the garage, which was open, by the way, just like my bedroom. And on the door of the car where the window was open, and on Edna herself."

He gave a grim half grin. "Despite what you see on TV, we don't usually print human skin or clothing unless we have no other choice. If there are other surfaces we can print, we go with those."

"Oh. Okay." I tried to think about where else he'd find prints. "The garage door opener on the wall will have my prints on it. But then my prints would be all over that anyway, along with Edna's. Probably even some of Dennis's if prints last that long."

"So that will be fairly smudged and probably unusable," he said. It sounded more like he was talking to himself, but since I wasn't exactly fully lucid right now it was hard to object.

"After I opened the door, I remembered Heather was still in the house. I got her out here to the patio and went and found the phone to call 911. Then I went back to check on Edna again. I was pretty sure she wasn't breathing. And I don't know CPR. I've been meaning to learn, the nurses at the Board and Care kept telling me it would be a good idea in case Dennis ever came home…" Okay, I was over the edge. Rambling now, and close to tears, and feeling awful.

Ray noticed. "I think I've got everything I need for the moment. Is there anything else you can think of that might be very important?"

Thankfully this time I remembered not to shake my head. "No. That's about it."

"Do you need a phone book or anything to make your calls?"

"There's a little notebook on my dresser. Should I get it, or do you want to?"

"I can get it. You just stay here." He sounded so kind for a change, I felt like crying even more. It was a side of this man I hadn't seen, at least not directed at me. Seeing it almost made me panic. Was I worse off than I thought? I pushed away the thought and just sat there, trying to get the landscape to settle down and not spin while I waited.

Fernandez brought me the notebook, and just about the time I started making the first call the crime scene techs got there and he excused himself to go deal with them. I could tell they were the crime scene people because their uniforms said just that.

I motioned for him to go on with them while I listened

to Linnette's phone ring until her answering machine picked up. It dawned on me then, while I was leaving a message, that she had said the night before that she'd be in the bookstore after five this morning.

I left that call until later and looked at what I'd jotted down for Pastor George. Fortunately I'd taken down his home number along with the church, and took a couple of deep breaths to steady myself and then called him at home. A sweet-sounding lady answered. The tone of her voice said she was used to calls at any time of day and wasn't fazed by someone calling her husband before breakfast.

I told him what was happening when he came to the phone, and it took a few moments for him to answer me. "That is terrible, Gracie Lee. Are you all right? And what about Heather?"

"Heather is already at the hospital. She went in the first ambulance. I'll be going in a few minutes, but I don't expect they'll keep me for long. I'm fine, really."

"Do you want someone else to deal with Dodd and Sons? I would be happy to do that for you."

"That would be great, Pastor." I could feel my shoulders sagging with relief at his suggestion. After last night I was ready to let somebody take over my complicated affairs anyplace they offered. "I'll get hold of Linnette Parks, and she will probably call the rest of the Christian Friends group. And the police will take care of notifying my husband's daughter about her grandmother."

"When you get to the hospital, put me on the list of people who are allowed to receive information about you. That way I'll know if they keep you or not, and where I should come to pray with you."

Oh, no. I was getting weepy again. "I will," I choked out. "And thank you for what you're doing already."

"Part of the job," he said softly before we said goodbye and he hung up.

I felt so surrounded by good people and God's love most of the time. This was another horrible situation, but amazingly, I was alive. Not only alive, but now that I was out in the fresh air, I was feeling much better. I said another quick prayer for Heather and her baby that they were all right, too. Then I looked in my notebook for the bookstore number.

I wasn't sure that anybody would pick up this time of day, but after quite a few rings, someone did. It wasn't Linnette, but one of the student workers, who agreed to go get her once I told him it was very important.

I didn't even explain the whole situation before she said "Oh, Gracie Lee, honey," with such sympathy that I immediately started crying. "I'm coming right over there," she said firmly.

"No, you're not." I put as much force behind my words as I could with a tight throat and a runny nose. "You'll call the rest of the Friends, get them all praying for Heather and the baby and go back to your inventory. Promise me."

She sighed. "Okay. But only because you aren't going to let me argue you out of this, I can tell. I'll be at the hospital as soon as I can do all this and get there. Don't try to tell me differently. Bye." And with that she hung up before we could negotiate anything else.

I sat there with the phone in my hand, trying to think if there was anything else I needed to do. This had left me even more confused than Dennis's death, and between the situation and being in the house full of fumes, I couldn't get my thoughts together.

Detective Fernandez was suddenly there beside me, making me jump. "Gracie Lee, the second ambulance is here. Is there a spare key to the house where you can get to it, so that I can make sure the doors are locked when I get done here?"

I knew there was, but remembering where took a moment. "The key is in that big stone pot right next to the front door, stuck in the dirt right next to the geranium."

He rolled his eyes. "Figures. Why hasn't this house been broken into before now?"

"I have no idea. I keep telling Edna…" That's as far as I got before it hit me. I wasn't going to keep telling Edna anything anymore. Once I started crying I didn't even argue with the ambulance personnel about getting on the gurney or anything. I sent one of them inside the house for my purse, which she found, and we left for the hospital. Under the oxygen mask they clapped on me almost immediately, I think I cried all the way there.

"Thankfully, we're this close to a hospital with a good emergency room," Linnette said as I started signing the paperwork that would let me out of Los Robles Hospital in nearby Thousand Oaks. It was only a seven-mile drive or thereabouts from Rancho Conejo. I was still feeling grumpy even though the E.R. personnel had pronounced me fit to leave.

"Yeah, but not good enough for them to keep Heather." I felt bad that she'd been whisked away to somewhere even bigger. She'd been through so much today that I felt like it was my fault.

"Gracie Lee, we've been over this already. It's not your fault. Pregnant women with suspected carbon monoxide poisoning are scary people for doctors. She may have looked good and felt stable, but nobody wanted to run the risk of the baby being poisoned, as well. And hyperbaric chambers are standard treatment for this kind of problem if you're pregnant."

Not being pregnant myself, a few hours of intense oxygen therapy had me ready to leave the hospital. Linnette had shown up by nine, assuring me that everybody was notified and praying and the bookstore inventory was in good hands. I'd told her what I knew about Heather, which wasn't much at that point besides she'd been transferred somewhere else, and she'd found out the rest.

"But they're pretty sure she'll be okay?"

"As sure as doctors ever are. Apparently they told Sandy that she'd be out by tonight, or possibly early tomorrow morning at the latest. She'll be there for Dennis's funeral, Gracie Lee. The doctors all but promised."

"Good. There's no way we can delay things again, and she'll want to be there. She went without knowing too long to have things end that way."

"And they won't," Linnette said firmly. "Now let me take you back to the house long enough for you to pack a bag, and we're going to Dot's."

"I don't know about that. I'll have to call the sheriff's department first and make sure that's all right."

"Don't bother. I already talked to Detective Fernandez, and he's the one who suggested that you stay someplace else. And since Dot had already offered you use of the apartment last night, I called her back and asked about putting you there temporarily tonight. She doesn't have any problem with it. She'd probably even lend you a dog to keep you company."

Now that sounded like a plan I could live with. "Then let's go pack that suitcase. I could use a furry hug," I told Linnette, savoring the bright sunshine that met us as the doors to the emergency room whooshed open to let us out.

By noon I was in the sparsely furnished apartment above Dot and Buck's freestanding garage. They lived out from Rancho Conejo a little bit off the main roads, into the hills where it was easy to imagine tumbleweeds rolling by in a drier time of year.

Back behind the main house there were half a dozen kennels with runs, and standing off to itself the four-car garage, with the apartment making a second story to the building. Stairs at the side of the building led to a balcony with a large picture window and the door to the apartment.

"I've been airing it out since Linnette called," Dot told us she led us up to the doorway. "It's not real fancy, but it's clean and it will do okay for tonight, I'm sure."

She rambled on as she ushered us in. "There's two bedrooms, but only one of them has furniture anymore, so I made up the bed in there for you, Gracie Lee. Even though nobody's lived here for close to four years, I still have a cleaning service do the bathroom and the kitchen once a month. When we get excess company we use it for housing, and we still keep saying we are going to rent it out."

It was a fairly compact apartment, but as advertised, it was clean and neat. The living room had a couch and a chair, a small television set and a set of three laminated coffee and end tables. Looking into the kitchen, I could see that past the divider that separated it with a high counter and stools from the living room, it was a simple galley with white appliances and a patterned vinyl floor showing at the doorway.

"There's the one bath." Dot flipped on the light. "That's the biggest drawback to renting someplace with two bedrooms, just having the one bath. It was okay for Candace and Susie, but for pickier renters they'd want at least a second half bath, anyway. And here's the bedroom."

Again, it was a small, tidy room. There was plenty of space for the single bed, a dresser, a wide closet and a bare desk. With a little fresh paint and a few knickknacks, it wouldn't have been half bad if you didn't mind green shag carpeting. Ben, with his penchant for retro, would have loved it.

At this point, it looked wonderful and I told Dot so. I got a hug in return, which brought me close to tears again. Almost everything was doing that in the past twenty-four hours.

"There isn't a phone line or cable," Dot said, sounding as if she were apologizing for not having the essentials instead of luxuries for an empty apartment.

"For one night, my cell phone and a radio will be just fine," I told her. "If I get lonely, Linnette told me you'd lend me a dog."

"You could have two if you really wanted them. Dixie has a sister who's due to have pups in about a week. We've been letting her sleep in the house in case anything happens early."

"I might take you up on that," I told her. It sounded better than being alone, even if I ended up delivering puppies at two in the morning. Watching new life being born would be better than watching what I'd seen today so far. Puppies were such great examples of God's creation and I could certainly use that kind of example.

In an hour I was ensconced in the apartment, having unpacked what little I'd brought over, and settled in to make calls on my cell phone. Dot insisted on bringing me soup and crackers for lunch, as well as some other essentials like milk and coffee, and I ate while I called my mom to give her the basics of the situation so that she could tell Ben. And, oh, yeah, I cried some more while I made the call. I really needed to find a brand of mascara that was truly waterproof if this kept up much longer.

I left a message with Jeannie at the detective division about where I was, and she promised to get the news to Ray. Helen at the church said she'd do the same for Pastor George, and added the word that she was sorry to hear about my latest troubles. Of course that brought on another need for waterproof mascara.

I'd finished my soup and my phone calls, and had nearly run out of tissues in the square box from the bathroom when there was a knock on the door. There was no peephole, but the view from the picture window was just wide enough to see Ray Fernandez at the door.

I let him in and showed him into the living room, such as it was. He stood near the doorway, looking a bit uncomfortable. "You're doing okay?"

"Well enough that the hospital let me out, obviously. What can you tell me about what you've found so far?"

"Not a whole lot. I do have a question, though," he said, settling down into the armchair. "Is there a reason that your mother-in-law would have, along with other papers, a copy of your life insurance policy? And did you just forget to tell me about it, or what?"

I couldn't imagine what he was talking about. "I only have one life insurance policy, for fifty thousand dollars. It was taken out a few years after Hal and I divorced, so that Ben would be taken care of if I died. He's the sole beneficiary. I can't imagine where Edna would have gotten a copy of it."

Ray showed me the paper. As I read it, I gasped. This policy was for a half-million dollars and it had been taken out a month before Dennis's accident…the accident that was supposed to kill me instead. The most twisted detail was that the policy named Edna as the beneficiary.

Ray sighed. "I figured you were going to say that. And it really makes everything so much more convoluted."

"Yes, but it looks like something I'd say Dennis would do, now that I know how he operated. He would have no problem forging my signature on the section saying that I knew about the policy. And making the beneficiary Edna instead of him made it appear less like this was a plan to make himself wealthy."

"The only thing Dennis would have needed would be an insurance agent willing to look the other way when he presented the policy already signed by you. I can see him being able to convince an agent it was an oversight."

"Especially if the agent was a woman." There was so much more we needed to talk about. "Let me put on a pot of coffee. I think we'll need it while we sort this out."

Ray nodded in agreement and I went to make coffee.

13

A few minutes later we settled in with the coffee and the folder of papers that Ray brought with him. "Okay, now I have to remind you, like I said before, this is a little outside regular procedure. Giving you this information goes against the way I normally do things anyway, but I need some answers to questions that I suspect only you can give me."

"I'll do anything I can. Did you get in touch with Becca?"

Ray nodded. "When I called earlier this morning, I reached her on her cell phone, and she was at her mother's. She agreed to stay there once I told her that the funeral was being delayed until tomorrow, and I got over there before noon. She seemed upset and surprised."

"Did either of them admit to knowing where Edna had been for over a week?"

"Not to me. After I met Becca there at her mother's I

started to regret having her stay there. It would have given them time to straighten out any kinks in their stories if they needed to do that."

I leaned forward. It was surprising to me that the detective might have come around to my way of thinking on this issue. "Was there anything in what they said that made you suspicious?"

"Nothing I could put my finger on. And while we know a lot more now from the note that Mrs. Peete left, where she's been since she left the Board and Care isn't one of the things we know from her." He stopped for a moment and took a drink of his coffee. "I thought you might want to know that when we processed the car, we found a small suitcase full of clothing in the trunk. You were right about the depression in the carpet."

I shrugged, feeling helpless instead of vindicated. "Not that it makes much difference now."

"Well, it confirmed what you told me. Now if you could look at this for a minute, I'd like you to tell me if this is your mother-in-law's handwriting." He pulled out several sheets of paper that looked like copies of a letter written on sheets of a legal pad.

The writing was easy to recognize. "It looks like her handwriting. That or someone was able to copy it surprisingly well."

"Since it was found next to her after a suicide attempt, we will at least start out assuming that it's her handwriting. The lab is looking at the originals for fingerprints and other information for us."

"Can I read this?" I looked at the folded sheets, noticing that he had shown me the second half of a page. I could only read parts of a couple sentences. It was enough to recognize Edna's handwriting, but not to see what she'd actually written.

He took it from me gently. "I'd rather you didn't. Can I ask you to trust me to tell you what it says?" His eyes were softer than they'd been most of the time I'd known this detective, and I got the funny feeling he was protecting me somehow. Remembering some of the things that Edna had said about other people in my presence, I could guess that he was probably trying to shield me from some unkind words about me.

I had to make a decision, and this one was easier than a lot of them I'd made over the last few days. "I have to trust you, Detective Fernandez. You've been straight with me so far."

He gave me a weak smile. "You might as well call me Ray. We've seen so much of each other now, and we're going to see plenty more of each other in the next two days."

This morning after I'd gotten out of the house, I remembered that he called me by my first name instead of Ms. Harris. It marked a change in our relationship, such as it was. I had to believe that this man no longer suspected me in any way of killing my husband. It was a relief.

"All right, Ray. So what does Edna's letter say?"

He took another sip of coffee, almost as if he wanted to put things off as long as possible. "It's not pretty. She says she gave Dennis the tea from your cup by mistake, thinking she'd picked up something else. Because of that, she takes full responsibility for killing her son and says she couldn't live with the knowledge."

"But why did she come back to the house to kill herself?"

Ray was looking down at the letter, and the surface of the coffee table. Anywhere, it seemed, but into my face. "That's the part I didn't want you to see. She said she was going back to the house to try and take you with her. Even though she took responsibility for Dennis's death because she gave him the tea, she was sure you were the one who'd put the drug in it and left it in the family waiting room as bait so that either she or Becca would drink it. And if you were dead, the only one who would benefit from the insurance policies would be Becca."

"Wait a minute. Insurance *policies?* I thought we were just talking about this one policy taken out on me. And even that one probably isn't valid."

"It isn't, but apparently she didn't know that, or at least pretended she didn't. And there's another policy taken out at the same time, on Dennis. She had it in the front seat with the rest of the papers, and some lawyer is going to have a field day with this one."

Now I was even more confused than before. "Why is that?"

Ray sighed. "Well, things are going to get awfully convoluted trying to sort all this out. Your husband's policy looks legitimate. But his mother is the beneficiary, and her note admits to killing him. So the insurance company would never have paid out the fifty thousand dollars on his policy to her."

I had to break in. "Fifty thousand? He insured me for half a million and himself for fifty thousand?"

Ray shrugged. "I have no idea. Maybe because he was cheap and would pay lower premiums on less insurance. Maybe he thought he was never going to die."

"That sounds like Dennis. And I guess we have to consider the possibility that you've been pushing all along. Maybe he was so intent on killing me after he insured me that the policy on him was just taken out to make mine look more legitimate." It was hard to suppress a shiver thinking about all this. "Why did you say there would be lawyers involved?"

"Because of one of the other pieces of paper Mrs. Peete had in the front seat. She basically cleaned out a file folder someplace with all her important papers, and put it next to that purse. The stack included her will, which left everything to Dennis, or if he did not survive her, his one and only daughter."

The light was beginning to dawn. "So Becca could have a lawyer argue that she should be entitled to the proceeds of her father's policy, since she didn't have anything to do with his death, and she is now the beneficiary by default."

"Exactly. And depending on what mood the court is in the day they argue this one, she could get her way."

I leaned back on the sofa, trying to digest all of this. "Do you think that's part of why Edna killed herself? I know she thought the world of Becca, and she would have done almost anything for her, I'm pretty sure."

Ray shook his head. "Hard to say. It's certainly possible that the insurance money could be a motive in her death. I imagine that, at the least, the papers we found in that front seat mean that this is going to be a matter for the courts from now on, not just a homicide detective."

He took another sip of his coffee and made the same face I would have made while drinking cold coffee. "I'll know more for sure once the full autopsy reports are in, but that will be several days. If there's a plus to any of this, it's that Mrs. Peete was also thoughtful enough to provide the paperwork she had concerning her funeral and Dennis's. She'd signed her copy, and Mr. Dodd says that's good enough for him to absolve you of most of the financial responsibility for tomorrow. And it gets her granddaughter out of paying for whatever services the family decides to have for Mrs. Peete, as well."

I felt tired and drained. "So does this mean the case is closed?"

Ray shook his head. "It means I can't do anything else until all of Mrs. Peete's autopsy reports are in."

That was certainly an enigmatic answer. It didn't sound like I was going to get anything clearer out of him. At this point, I wasn't going to try and push for more, either. "Will you be at the services tomorrow, Ray?"

"Definitely. I don't subscribe to the theory that says startling revelations are likely to happen there, and in this case that's a good thing, because I think we've had all the revelations we're going to get right here." He tapped the papers resting on the coffee table. "Still, I need to put some closure on all this for myself. And for you, I expect, and Ms. Taylor and the rest of that group you've gotten involved in."

"The Christian Friends," I told him. "And maybe you might even want to say a few words to Ms. Taylor." *Like*

an apology, I felt like saying, but didn't. I'd started calling the detective by his first name. No sense in losing
ground again.

He got up from the armchair, and I got up, as well. "I
just might want to do that, as long as it waits until tomorrow," he admitted. "Seems like I've been spending way
too much time today admitting I was wrong. I can save
a few of those confessions for another day."

He gathered up his paperwork, thanked me for the coffee and left. And I sat in the mostly empty apartment and
thought for a while, wishing I had my computer to instant message with Ben for a while.

Instead I took Dot up on her offer of taking a dog for
a while. In the end I settled for Hondo, because Dixie
didn't want to leave Dot's side, and her sister was too
heavy with pups to make it up the stairs to the apartment.
Hondo, however, would go anywhere that someone was
willing to scratch behind his ears and tell him what a
grand guy he was, and I had plenty of time for that.

So I sat for a couple hours, thinking a lot and scratch-
ing behind Hondo's ears while he moaned in pleasure as
only a happy dog can do. It gave me plenty of time to consider the way Dennis's death had happened. It struck me
as incredibly sad that Edna had been the one to cause his
death. It was even sadder that she'd stewed over that
knowledge for a week and then killed herself, trying to
kill me in the process. And for a reason that I knew was
false. Had she drugged that tea and blamed me, or did
someone else?

Hondo listened while I talked about some of this out
loud. It was one of those funny conversations, half prayer

and half just trying to work things out for myself. Only when it had gotten dark that evening did the two of us head for the main house to have dinner with Dot and Buck.

I stayed at the main house for quite a while after dinner, not wanting to go back to be alone. Buck and Dot suggested I take Hondo back with me, but he looked so happy where he was by Buck's feet that I didn't want to move him. So in the end I went back to the apartment by myself. At least I slept there by myself. Buck insisted on checking things out before I settled in for the night.

It was really weird waking up Saturday morning in yet another strange bed. For a moment I panicked, trying to figure out where I was and what was happening. Then I lay back down against the pillows, telling myself that everything was okay. For a change I could believe that God was really in control. It was definitely much better compared to yesterday morning, even though this apartment was a strange place I wasn't used to being.

I looked at my watch on the bedside table, and was surprised to see that I'd slept through until eight in the morning. I got up quickly then so that I could get ready for the long day ahead.

Some of the things from the last tenants were still here, like a little plaque on the bathroom wall that said, This Is The Day The Lord Has Made… Rejoice! I had to admit I didn't feel much like rejoicing right now, but when it came down to it there was plenty to rejoice about. I was still here, and after today my life was likely to get much better by leaps and bounds.

Of course there was still today to get through, and as I got the shower water going, it was difficult to decide which part of today was going to be the most challenging.

I went out for coffee once I was dressed and ready for the funeral, being careful that I didn't spill any part of my latte on the pewter-gray dress and jacket I'd chosen for the day. The only black ensemble in my closet back at the house had been a pantsuit that looked a little too trendy for my husband's funeral, so I decided that cut was more important than color and went with the more conservative dress.

The jacket that went with the sheath had one more advantage: it had good-sized, well-cut pockets that didn't bag out when I loaded them with plenty of tissues and my cell phone. I didn't expect calls today, but at the same time I'd gotten to the point where I felt kind of naked without the silly thing. Maybe I really was becoming a Californian, after all.

"You rubbed off on me in a lot of ways, Dennis," I said, talking to him for the first time since he'd died. I'd done it all the time in the months when he'd lain comatose in the care center. It had become a habit, whether I was really there or not.

When he was in the care center, the nurses had said that he could probably hear most of what was going on, even though he was far from communicating back. Now that he was dead I hoped he couldn't hear anything I said to him. And in the most perverse way, I really hoped he was with Jesus, even though I was far from happy about the myriad situations he'd left here on earth for me to clean up. While I knew now that Dennis had lived an entirely different life here on earth than the one I'd known about, I hoped there was a third life, as well, one that included the Lord in ways the rest of us just couldn't see.

I was at Dodd and Sons now and had to stop conversing with dead people. It just wasn't done in some places, unless one wanted to be looked on as downright dotty, as Granny Lou would have said. And though I'd been through a lot in the past few weeks, I was hardly to that point yet.

It was early for anyone else to be there, so it wasn't surprising when Scott Dodd and another gentleman in a dark suit were the only ones near the door of the chapel. "I'm glad to see you, Ms. Harris," he said, coming up with hand outstretched. "And I have to tell you that I'm so sorry about Mrs. Peete. Detective Fernandez told me all that he could about the situation. I fully understand why we had to postpone things until today."

That was good. The last thing I needed was aggravation from the funeral director. I hadn't seen any cars in the parking lot that looked familiar, but I thought I'd ask. "Is anyone else here yet in the way of family or friends?"

"Not yet. I understand that Mr. Peete's daughter should be here soon, along with her mother. We spoke to his daughter last night and she had some suggestions on family seating." He ushered me into the chapel, where I could see that the front row on both sides of the chapel had been roped off in heavy purple roping and had Reserved signs.

Every effort had been made to set things up in the exact middle of the front of the chapel with flower arrangements flanking the pedestal where a simple urn sat. I had a feeling I knew what was coming even before

Scott pointed it out. "I suspect that Becca doesn't want to sit in the same pew with me, and especially not with Ms. Taylor. Am I right?"

Scott unconsciously ran a finger around the collar of his white shirt. "That's about the size of it. Do you mind if she and her mother sit on one side of the aisle and you and Ms. Taylor sit on the other?"

"Not at all. If Mrs. Peete were still with us, I suspect she might have suggested this, anyway. As long as we're all in the front row, I don't think it matters where in that front row we sit. This will make things much calmer on an already-uncomfortable day."

Scott looked visibly relieved. "Good." He motioned toward the display at the front of the chapel, back to being efficient and in control of the situation. "We took the liberty of adding a few floral displays to what was ordered. And I appreciate the picture that you gave us. I had it blown up slightly so that our guests could remember Mr. Peete at his best."

It had been a good photo of Dennis, and looked even better expanded and in an eight-by-ten frame positioned on a stand near the pedestal with the urn. There wouldn't be any collage of snapshots like I'd seen at some funerals where folks had chosen cremation or a closed casket. There just weren't enough candid photos of Dennis, or Jack, or whatever he called himself in different situations, to make a collage. I don't think he'd gone in for candid shots in about twenty years. Definitely I'd never seen any, making me muse again about how little I'd known about this man when I married him. For that matter I didn't know that much more about him now that our relationship was at its finish.

* * *

The one flaw in the plan to keep the "families" separated became apparent shortly after Becca and her mom came into the chapel. Heather and I had parked ourselves in front of the pew we'd be occupying, and Carol and Becca, juggling Ollie between them, had done the same. Heather had beaten them to the funeral home by about ten minutes, her mother apparently having driven her there. Sandy hung near the back of the room and Heather came up to the front with me. She hadn't said much, giving me curt answers to my questions about how she was feeling. I decided not to press things. She'd been through quite a bit in the past twenty-four hours and probably felt like most of it was my fault.

Soon others began coming in and I watched each group stand at the back of the chapel, trying to figure out where to go first so that they wouldn't offend anybody but talk to both sets of people. Anybody who knew both Becca and me was faced with a little social dilemma here that wouldn't be easy for them to solve: how to greet both of us without offending anybody by going one place first.

I thought about just sidling over next to Becca to solve the dilemma, but knew it wouldn't work. The one time I got even three feet closer to her, beginning to bridge the gap across the main aisle, she slid over the same amount of distance without even looking at me. So much for that move.

Finally I shrugged it off, telling myself that this was only for an hour, and there wouldn't be that many people involved to begin with. The Christian Friends members, even Paula, filtered into the chapel and came over to hug both Heather and me. Heather was a little more outgoing with them, but still somewhat more reserved than usual.

The church folks were perfectly pleasant to Becca, as well, making me proud of all of them. After a few minutes Carol sat over to the side, taking care of her wiggly grandson. Ollie was having a good time standing on the carpet in stockinged feet, wanting to spend most of his time balancing with help from an adult. Soon he'd be standing alone and then walking, and I didn't envy his mother and grandmother the task of keeping up with him then.

Pastor George came in shortly after Carol and Becca, and spent most of his time in discussion with one or another of us. I imagined he was gathering last-minute information so that he could say all the right things about Dennis. I saw him pause several times to add to notes he had taken on cards he put in a front pocket of his black suit. How, I wondered, did a minister preach a funeral for someone like Dennis, who hadn't been a church member and presented so many challenges? I didn't envy the good pastor a moment of the task ahead of him.

The room filled slowly over the course of an hour. It was going to be a fairly sparse service, but I didn't expect anything different. Besides the Christian Friends and Heather's mom, there were a few people I remembered seeing from Conejo Chapel on "our" side of the room, and a few I didn't recognize who spoke with Becca or her mother and slipped into seats on "their" side afterward.

Sam Blankenship from the newspaper showed up, being as discreet as possible with his notebook and pen.

He came up to talk to everyone, and I thought he looked nicer than I'd seen him before. His shirt and tie might have come from a thrift store, but they were clean and pressed. A small delegation from the Conejo Board and Care came in, mostly not speaking to anybody in the front of the room but finding seats midway back or farther in the pews. Among one group I noticed Adela Rodriguez and the young woman who'd gone with her to the sheriff's department. I was a little surprised to see her at first, but not when I really thought about it. She probably went to the funerals of most of the people who died at the Board and Care. I would have, given her job, and she struck me as a caring person much like the Christian Friends members.

When the music had started, a few minutes before eleven, I noticed Ray Fernandez slide into one of the pews near the back. He caught my eye and gave a curt nod. In his dark sport coat he looked like one of the doctors from the care center or any of the other men there, and fit right in.

I started needing my tissues just moments after Pastor George got up to speak. He did a great job of relating to everybody there without saying one compromising thing about Dennis. I knew how difficult that was, and so did quite a few people there. A few of them would probably have been happier if he'd let rip and said all the compromising things he could about Dennis, but today I wasn't in that camp.

Looking down the aisle at the women assembled there, it was another reminder of Dennis and his choices. Carol was farthest from me, holding her grandson. The baby had even paler blond hair than his mother, and I wondered again what Becca's husband, Brandon, looked like.

Looking at them and then at Heather on my other side, who was getting pretty upset by now, it could have been some slightly odd family reunion where I fit right in. We all were wearing shades of gray or dark blue, and our build and hair coloring certainly could have made us relatives. Instead, we were all related by our odd relationships to this man we were putting to rest today. Pulling my concentration back to the pastor, I listened to his sermon.

He was really making me think about things in a new and different way while he spoke about Dennis, and Edna, and why so much happens that is totally beyond our control and our understanding. He talked about the pain in my husband's life, that he'd made mistakes but still his family cared for him. Edna had cared the most, but in light of recent events, the pastor didn't bring that up. It still made me hurt to think that she'd been the one to give him the drink that had killed him. She would never have done that intentionally, and it pained me to think she couldn't live with the knowledge of what she'd done. It stung even worse to know how much anger she tried to vent on me because she thought I was responsible for Dennis's death in the first place.

The pastor went on to say more about Dennis and what we didn't know about his life, tying into his message about God's place in our fallen, broken world. I looked over across the aisle to see how Becca and Carol were handling all this. They were doing okay, but Ollie was starting to lose his patience. He was facing backward on the pew, holding himself up and bouncing up and down, just able to boost himself over the edge to see the row behind him, which was empty. One of those bounces made him knock his drooly chin against the hard wooden pew and he started to wail.

I winced at the sound his chin made in contact with the wood, as did his grandmother. His mother picked him up and patted him for a moment. Conscious of her place in the front row when he built up to a howl, she stood and jiggled him for a while. When he subsided a little, she sat down, with him standing in her lap as he wound down.

I totally lost the thread of what Pastor George was talking about just as he started saying we could all hold on to the hope that Dennis had repented at the end. Instead, I watched Becca get up and down with the baby. The pants and top that she wore were probably the best she owned, or at least the best she could fit into right now. She hadn't exactly regained her figure in the eight months since her son was born.

Of course I didn't know where she'd started out before pregnancy, but kind of guessed that she'd been in a little better shape before having a baby took its toll. While I was still watching her, trying not to stare, Ollie decided to rev up his howling to full blast and she stood up one more time to get him settled. This time it worked, but not before her moving around in the pew gave me an unsettling idea.

That idea had started growing a few minutes before, when I'd looked at all of us ranged down the row, and our similar appearance. Watching Becca now, the idea blossomed into fullness and I couldn't shake it. The more I looked at her, the more I was sure that anybody seeing her from the back only, say walking down a hallway, would have said that she was probably pregnant.

Her hair color was similar to Heather's, maybe a shade or two lighter, and it was close to the same length. Both women tended to wear their hair pulled back in a ponytail, although neither had chosen that style today.

Pastor George had finished his remarks, and Heather was gently nudging me and hissing my name. Apparently he had asked the "family" to leave the chapel first and go to the back of the room. Still trying not to stare at Becca, I got up and did what Heather told me to, my mind in a whirl.

"Do you think everybody will come back to the church for the luncheon he just told them about?" Heather asked quietly as we went down the aisle.

"I don't know. I hope most of them do." I particularly hoped two of them would—Becca and Ray Fernandez—because I wanted to talk to both of them at the same time about the idea that was growing into certainty as the strains of familiar hymns played around me in the chapel. I wanted to see what Becca said about my idea. "You're going, aren't you?" I asked Heather.

"Sure. Right. I wouldn't miss it for the world. And then I am going someplace all by myself and celebrating being done with this entire bunch of people forever." She turned away from me without another word.

Wow. That put a bit of a different spin on what I'd been thinking about. Maybe I couldn't be so certain about

Becca, after all. I kept my distance from all three of the other "family" members as everyone left the chapel, wondering what I was supposed to do now.

14

Now I was really stuck. Before Heather's little outburst I was sure that I should confront Becca in the church hall, or at least bounce my theory off the Christian Friends, and then tell Ray what was going on in my mind and see what he thought about it. But then Heather got me all confused again, and there I stood in the church hall, wondering what to do. I still thought I should talk to Becca. Maybe Heather was just being hormonal and pregnant.

It didn't help that I couldn't find anybody I knew and trusted among the women setting out ham, salads and slices of Bundt cake on the serving tables in the room set up for the luncheon. If I'd seen Linnette right away, or even Dot, to provide me with some grounding, I would have been okay. At this point I might have even taken advice from Paula, which proved how desperate I was. Instead I just stood there, trying to figure out what to do next. An older lady with blue-rinsed hair kept urging me to start through the buffet line, which was the last thing I felt like doing.

I did go over to the giant coffeepot in the corner and poured myself a cup of coffee. It would be decaf here, I knew, so I didn't have to worry about getting too jazzed while I waited. The doctors, nurses and others from Conejo Board and Care, and various people from the church were filtering in, but not Linnette or Dot. Sandy came in, steering Heather along, but I didn't feel like getting into a conversation with her again quite so soon.

So much for what I wanted, because the minute Heather saw me, she broke away from her mother and came over in my direction. "Gracie Lee, I'm so sorry for snarling at you back there." She looked like she was close to tears. "I don't know what's wrong with me today. I'm in such a horrible mood. Maybe that hyperbaric chamber messed me up while it was giving me all the good oxygen for the baby."

She hugged me as tightly as she could with her belly between us, and as she did so I could feel the baby kick. "Wow, at least we know he or she is still healthy," I said, both of us laughing at the odd sensation.

"That's such a relief. I was so scared when they put me in that ambulance."

"And I felt so bad because I was the one who made you stay. If I'd just been able to get my act together and stay alone Thursday night, you wouldn't have had to go through that."

Heather shrugged. "Hey, I decided to stay. Nobody twisted my arm."

I looked over near the buffet tables where Sandy was standing, looking at us intensely. "Well, your mom looks like she might want to twist mine if I don't let you go back next to her and get something to eat. I'll talk to you later, okay?"

"Fine." She waved and headed in her mom's direction. I felt like a weight had lifted off my shoulders, knowing that Heather was just in one of those late-pregnancy mood swings. Everything she'd been through certainly would bring them on. Of course I remembered when I'd gotten the crabbiest in late pregnancy, but I didn't want to add to her burdens by suggesting that she might be in early labor. And since everyone is different, I held my tongue.

Now I'd finished most of my coffee, and the rest of my friends still weren't in evidence. Neither was Ray. Then Carol came out of the ladies' room with Ollie and a tote bag, looking for a place to sit down, and my decision about what to do next was made by seeing her. I wondered how I'd missed her, and probably Becca, going in there in my concentration on finding everybody. Maybe it had happened when I was talking to the Blue Rinse Lady or hugging Heather. Meanwhile Carol found a high chair and started settling her rambunctious grandson into it while he protested that idea.

Taking a deep breath, I went over to where she was finishing buckling the last strap as she talked to the baby. "Hi, Carol. Thank you for coming. I know it was a comfort to Becca to have you there today."

She looked over her shoulder. "In a really weird sort of way, it was a comfort to me, too. It puts a cap on things this way. Most things, anyway. I guess we'll go through this again in a couple days when we bury Edna." She shook her head. "What she did sure came out of the blue. Did you ever figure out where she'd been?"

Either she was a better actor than I would have expected, or she really had no idea where Edna had spent her time once she'd walked out of Dennis's room at Conejo Board and Care. "Not really. And she certainly didn't say in her note."

Becca hadn't followed her out of the ladies' room, and looking around the room, I didn't see her anywhere else. "Where did Becca get to?"

"I don't know," she said, with less conviction than she'd put in her earlier statement. "I'm sure she'll turn up in a minute or two." She started sorting through the diaper bag, but came out empty-handed in a minute.

"Can I get you something while we wait for her?" I hated to see her just sitting here with the baby, who was starting to fuss a little faced with an empty high chair tray.

She gave a noncommittal "Sure," and I took it as license to go fill a plate with different things from the table, along with a cup of coffee, and bring it back to the table where she sat.

She looked truly thankful when I brought the food back. "I made certain to get a few things that I thought Ollie could eat, depending on how far along he is on solids," I told her.

"Great, because the cereal Becca packed ran out in the car coming over here. Sometimes she doesn't think ahead much," she said, shaking her head. She handed Ollie a cracker and he stopped fussing immediately and watched while she broke up a few other things into bits and fished a couple of fat green peas out of one of the salads for him, decorating the tray.

Carol looked around the room and motioned for me to sit next to her. "I probably shouldn't tell you this, but I don't totally agree with what Becca was doing, so I will. I know exactly where she is. She dropped me off here because she said she wanted some time alone at Edna's house. But I think what she really wanted was some time alone with her grandmother's jewelry case and silver drawer before you thought about going back to the house."

She busied herself with a little more food for Ollie, and I held my breath, waiting to see if she had more to say. "I don't think you're the kind of person who would really want any of my daughter's inheritance, or at least what she sees as her inheritance. And you seem anxious to talk to her. If that's the case, you can probably catch her at Edna's."

"I'll do that. Thanks for telling me," I said. I got up from the table where Carol was finally cutting a few bites of food for herself along with feeding the baby. Looking around the room, I still couldn't find Ray Fernandez. Of all the times for him to totally disappear, this was the worst.

I looked at the clock high on one wall. It had been forty-five minutes since we'd left Dodd and Sons. It wasn't likely that Becca would spend too much time at her grandmother's. If I wanted to catch her there, I'd have to hurry.

At least she left the baby with her mother, I told myself as I drove, as fast as I could, over to the house. Maybe Becca had more sense than I credited her for, and less criminal intent. She might just be a somewhat shallow twenty-two-year-old young woman, afraid her evil step-mother was going to get Edna's jewelry before she did. Not that I could think of a thing of Edna's I'd really have wanted, but I wouldn't be able to convince her of that.

And there was still the chance that I'd been arguing against all along, that Heather was the one who'd put the GHB in my tea. At that point she could have had several reasons to be angry with me. After all, I'd had the place by right that she thought she deserved. She could have even seen me as the reason that Dennis was in such a bad way to begin with; if he hadn't been racing back toward the house, and me, he wouldn't have been injured. She certainly had surprised me today; maybe the side of her that I'd seen at Dodd and Sons was what had been hidden all along.

I tried out all those arguments on the short drive to the house, but couldn't really convince myself of any of them. It was even less convincing when Becca's little car was out in front of the house. It was actually parked next door, but I recognized the slightly battered little sedan plastered with skateboarding bumper stickers, Ollie's car seat in the back seat.

She'd locked the front door behind her, too. I tried the knob just to make sure, but nothing happened when I turned it. I fished out my keys, unlocking the door and stepping into the hall. "Becca? It's Gracie Lee," I called, not wanting to startle her. Apparently that plan didn't work, because something hard hit me on the head after that, and as the lights went out I thought to myself through the fog that I should have made more noise coming in so I wasn't mistaken for a burglar.

* * *

Sometime later I came to with the worst headache I'd ever had. For one brief panicky moment I thought I'd been paralyzed by the blow to the head, because I was sitting up somewhere, but couldn't move around. Then I looked down and saw that I was sitting at my desk chair near the computer, with clothesline wrapped around me from shoulders to elbows.

There was noise around me of someone rattling through the house. Drawers were being opened and closed, and from the sounds I could hear, maybe even being dumped out. I could hear closet doors open and close. My head throbbed and I was so confused. I had come in here with a purpose, I knew, but just now I couldn't remember what it was.

After a few minutes, still listening to the noise of what sounded like rooms being turned upside down, I remembered that I'd come here looking for Becca. But where was she? Before I'd been suspicious of her, but maybe I had been wrong about that. Maybe I had interrupted a burglary after all. She could be tied up someplace, too, while someone else ransacked the house.

Just then she came around the corner into the living room, carrying a pillowcase that looked as if it was loaded with something. "Becca. I'm so glad you're not hurt," I said.

"Wish I could say the same about you. Boy, Gracie, you have the worst luck. Almost as bad as mine. First I come in here to make sure that you hadn't cleaned out my grandma's stuff and I surprise a couple of burglars. Then you get here to prove me right, but before you can take anything they get you, too. It's a shame they're going to shoot you."

While she talked to me, Becca went around the room dumping things into her pillowcase and creating little bits of havoc. She knocked over Edna's favorite philodendron, spewing dirt over the carpet, and snagged a silver picture frame with a picture of Dennis, stuffing it in the pillowcase sack.

It was hard to understand what she was talking about. Where were the burglars? And what was she talking about, saying somebody was going to shoot me? Now that she was in the room with me, I couldn't hear noises anywhere else. "Shouldn't we be leaving if there are burglars? Why don't you just untie me and we can both get out of here?" I asked.

She gave a short ugly laugh. "Maybe I hit you on the head harder than I thought. Or maybe you're dumber than I imagined, although I can't figure how that could happen. You certainly are harder to kill than I ever thought you would be."

My head hurt so much, and what she was saying didn't make any sense. I tried to struggle out of the chair again, but in addition to my arms being tethered, my feet were tied up with something at the ankles, and there was no way to move. "What…what do you mean?" I finally asked her.

"Oh, man. You really are denser than I thought. There are no burglars here, Grace. But that's what I'm going to tell everybody when I get out of here and you don't." She shook her head and went about sorting through the living room.

"If you went for the burglar act, that must mean you bought that story about Grams feeding Daddy the tea all by herself, didn't you? I know the cops did, because that big Latino one already saw me at the funeral, and he was just as nice as anything. Said how sorry he was for my loss. Right, some loss. More like a gain of a quarter million dollars."

I felt cold and numb all over now, even in my fingers where I could wiggle a little bit. Was that because of the tightness of the cords binding me or the growing shock of what Becca was saying? Becca was still wandering around the house, making it look like someone had burglarized it. I noticed that anything that caught her eye went into the pillowcase. "What I can't believe," she said, moving on to the dining room and snatching up a small vase Edna kept on a shelf, "is that so quickly Grams bought what I was telling her. It was easy enough to convince her that either you or Daddy's latest fling dosed the tea. But by that night I had her convinced that she was a murderer."

"Why? Your dad was the last person on earth your grandmother would want to harm." Maybe if I kept her busy, Becca wouldn't notice how much I was trying to get out of the cords that bound me. I couldn't see anything that would help me get out of the cords, but out of the corner of my eye I could tell that the bottom of my computer screen was flashing. That usually meant something, but try as I might, I couldn't remember what. Remembering almost anything more challenging than my name was so hard right now, with the throbbing in my head.

"Hey, the good silver. I didn't know Grams still had this," Becca said with glee. Her words were a little muffled because her head was deep in the open sideboard in the dining room. "I really thought Dad had conned her out of this for one of his companies. He was so good at that."

She wiggled backward out of the sideboard, a heavy cloth pouch in her hands. "I'm going to need another pillowcase. Cool." Putting down the silver on the table, she headed back toward the bedrooms, giving my chair a little spin as she passed. The motion made me gag.

"Don't wear yourself out trying to get out of there. I tied you up really tight. And since I used all the phone cords, you won't have to be concerned about calling for help, either. Those burglars, they think of everything." With a sinking feeling, I looked down and saw that she was telling the truth—the cords I'd mistaken for clothesline were the telephone cords.

The flashing was still going on at the bottom of the computer screen, and I made my head hurt even worse by trying to remember what that meant. Contact of some kind, didn't it? That flashing signaled messages. Some kind of messages that had their own phone line that Becca wouldn't have messed with. Instant messages, that's what they were called. It finally came to me and I stretched my fingers as much as possible to try and reach the mouse. I got it, and clicked on that little flashing part of the bar. A box popped up on the screen. It was Ben! He was home from school and had sent me an instant message just a few minutes ago.

Please, God, let him still be at the computer, I prayed fervently as I read his message. "Hi, Mom. U there? I have way cool news."

His news, whatever it was, would have to wait. I could hear Becca coming back up the hall, and as quickly as possible, clicked the mouse again to hide the message.

The motion of turning away from the computer again made me even more dizzy and nauseated, but I did it. "Got two while I was at it." Becca brandished her grandmother's prize embroidered pillowcases. "And once I fill them up, we have to get this show on the road, Gracie. See, these burglars are not only really good at what they do, using gloves and all so they don't leave fingerprints," she said, waving her plastic-encased fingers at me, "but they are also really mean. They don't want to leave any witnesses, which is why they're going to shoot both of us. Fortunately they're just going to wing me and I'm going to play dead until they leave. But you're going to be past hope."

This time I understood what she was saying and it made me tremble. "Why bother? You are already in so much trouble, Becca. Why kill me, too?"

"Oh, that one's easy. For the insurance money. There's a cool quarter million dollars waiting for me when you die. See, I'm Grams's only heir, and she was in line to get money from the policy." She looked around the room as she leaned against the kitchen doorway. "Guess I'll get the house, too. Man, I'm redoing the kitchen before we move in, even if it means living in that crummy apartment another six months."

I had to get her out of the living room and keep her busy, even if it was just for a few minutes. "If it's money you need, I can tell you where there is some. I'll bet you didn't know that your grandma kept cash in the pantry."

"I'd forgotten about that. She used to have cash in that fake flour tin years ago, and more in a baking powder one. You mean Dad never cleaned those out?"

This felt like it was buying me precious minutes. "If he did, she loaded them back up. Last time I saw her with one of the tins, it had at least a hundred dollars in it."

Becca laughed her ugly laugh again. "And you've been here over a week without her and you didn't touch it. You are so much dumber than I thought."

She went into the kitchen and I heard the pantry open. I knew that Edna's money tins were back in the far reaches of the pantry, and prayed that the hunt would keep Becca busy long enough. The moment I heard the pantry open I turned back around and clicked the mouse again. Ben had sent me another message. "Mom? U there?"

I typed as fast as I could with the fingers on my right hand that would reach the keyboard by stretching as far as I could. I hit the Caps Lock key for speed and emphasis and typed: "HERE. NEED HLP. CALL RAY NOW. SEND HERE ASAP. I LV U, BEN." Then I pushed Send. Realizing that I wasn't hearing much noise in the kitchen, I closed the instant message window, then hid the screen again and turned around so that when Becca came into the room all she saw was me fiddling with my bonds.

"I told you, they aren't going to give," she said, sounding tired. "And that was smart, you telling me about the money in the kitchen. Good burglars would have found that. It adds another creative touch to this whole thing.

Besides, it almost covers the cab fare I had to pay to get back to Sherman Oaks last night. Too bad I have to shoot you anyway."

It was hard to take in everything she said. She looked so glassy-eyed and hyped up that it made me wonder if Becca was high on something, or if she just really enjoyed the adrenaline rush that this kind of danger gave her. Either way, I couldn't think of any way to reason with her at this point. I was still so foggy from being hit on the head. Maybe if I had a little more time I would come up with a plan. At least she didn't have a gun in her hand yet. Maybe she didn't really have one.

As if she read my mind, Becca put down the pillowcase and reached around to the back of the waistband of her pants. The gun she pulled out looked small, but efficient. "And you thought I was kidding," she said with an evil grin. "I'm not. See, it was right here waiting for me to use in a couple minutes, once I make sure that all the good stuff is packed up and ready to go."

She made one more sweep of the living room and wandered down the hall, talking as she went. "You're not saying anything more, Gracie. Why not? Usually you're so talkative. Daddy always said he thought you were going to talk his ear off." I could hear something go into the pillowcase she'd picked up again. "Hey, what do you think of one last gabfest? After the burglars shoot us both, and you know you're dying and all, I think you're going to talk to me. See, you knew about Heather after all, which is why you ran your own car off the road that night with Daddy driving it. And when that didn't do the trick and Daddy started waking up, you couldn't have

that because he'd tattle on you. So you slipped him a little something you thought would slow down the process,
but it killed him instead. What a relief for you that Grams
fed him the tea and did your dirty work for you."

"That's terrible. Nobody will believe that."

"Hey, they've believed me up until now," she said as if
she were talking about a parking ticket she'd weaseled
out of, not two murders and two attempts at more.

She put all the loaded pillowcases in a pile and looked
out the window nearest the front door. "Coast is clear.
I'll go put these in the trunk. You say your prayers while
I'm gone, because this is it. I'm so glad the burglars are
going to take that lousy beater with them. I need a new
car almost as bad as I need this house."

She was out the door and I made one last effort to get
out of the cords that held me. It didn't work, but I wasn't
going to just sit here and let this deranged young woman
shoot me, because I knew she would. I couldn't budge
the cords around my arms, but with a lot of effort, I got
one foot down to the floor. By throwing my weight from
one side of the chair to the other and pushing with that
foot, I could move the chair.

I'd gotten a good ten feet by the time I heard the car
trunk slam and Becca come up the front walk. She'd left
the front door locked behind her again, and it gave me
a few more wonderful seconds to wriggle even farther toward the front door, moving to the side of the front hallway away from the side of the door that opened.

"Okay, showtime," she crooned when she got the door
open. She stood one step past the doorway, looking at
where she left me. "Hey, where'd you go…?"

In that one moment of surprise, I gave it all I had. Screaming as loudly as I could, I launched the whole chair at her, praying she was a lousy shot. We tumbled into a heap on the floor and the gun went off just as I heard sirens outside the open door. My ears were ringing so loudly from the noise and the motion that I couldn't do anything but retch and pray that it would take just enough time for Becca to crawl out from under me that the police could make it to the door. At least the movement had knocked the gun out of her hand. I could see it on the tile floor of the hallway, where Becca was groping for it.

Ray Fernandez was the sweetest thing I'd ever seen, even with a gun drawn and a look of panic on his face. Becca must have seen him about the same time that I did, because she gave a mighty effort and heaved the chair—and me with it—off of her body. The motion hit my head against the wall next to the front door, and the pain put me down for the count.

15

They told me later that once Ray and his backup uniformed officers from the sheriff's department arrested Becca they called the paramedics again. I took my second ambulance ride in two days back to Los Robles Hospital, even though I didn't ever remember that part of the commotion. I do remember having a conversation with one of the doctors later in the day, who said that retrograde amnesia was a tricky thing.

Apparently getting hit on the head often means that you lose little chunks of memory around the event. Getting whomped twice in the course of an hour, I was probably extremely lucky that the only thing I "lost" was an ambulance ride with my friend Steve and company and a bit of time in the emergency room at Los Robles.

I would have liked to have lost some of the time I spent with Becca there at the house. Although I guess it was good that I could tell Ray Fernandez all about what she'd said once he talked to me that evening in my hospital room. The doctors insisted on keeping me overnight due to the concussion I'd received. At that point I was sore and felt awful and couldn't really argue with their decision.

"Now why didn't you just wait for me to show up at the church instead of going off after Becca?" Ray did not look at all happy. "It would have made life so much easier for everybody."

"You were coming to the church? Could have fooled me," I countered. "I waited around at least half an hour hoping to talk to you."

"I was busy talking to Adela Rodriguez after she stopped me in the parking lot at Dodd and Sons. She was almost certain she'd made a positive ID on the person she'd seen leaving Dennis's room during the funeral, but she felt so bad about what she had to tell me that she waited until the family was gone."

"Because the person she identified was Becca? I thought the same thing, and it's what I wanted to tell you at the church. When Carol told me that Becca was at the house going through her grandmother's things, I thought I'd confront her there."

Ray folded his arms and stood at the side of my bed, scowling. "Do you realize how silly that sounds? Gracie Lee, she could have killed you. She almost did."

"I know that now. At the time I really thought that her involvement might have only stretched to hustling her grandmother out of there, and putting the GHB in my tea."

"Wouldn't that be enough to stop you?"

I shrugged. "It should have been, I guess. At least things turned out okay. Remind me to never give my son any grief again about how much time he spends on the computer." Ben had been the first person I'd talked to once I could use a phone in the hospital. Our conversation had been somewhat stilted, and along the same lines of the one I was having with Ray, with my son pointing out to me how much danger I'd been in and how foolish I'd been to go to the house alone. "I'm also thankful to you that you called him the moment you could, to tell him everything was okay."

"Hey, he was worried about you. That was one panicked young man I talked to while I was on my way to that house."

"You were already on your way?"

"I told you, I showed up at the church," Ray said, speaking slowly and distinctly as if to a small child. I couldn't fault him for that, because I was pretty sure that folks had been repeating themselves around me all day. "Once I found out that Becca was at the house and you'd gone after her, do you think I would have gone anywhere else?"

"I guess not. Especially if you'd talked to Señora Rodriguez." It seemed odd that in the end everything had turned on a case of mistaken identity, corrected during Dennis's funeral. This whole series of events that led to Dennis's death and to Edna's seemed to hinge on such small things.

That reminded me of something else I needed to tell Ray. "I think Becca was the one who ran her father off the road back in August. Of course then she thought it was me. She said something at the house that made me think she'd done it, anyway."

He nodded. "I read the young lady her rights the moment I arrested her, because she was so mad at you that she wanted to talk. According to her everything that happened was your fault. You were supposed to be driving your own car that day, so that the scheme she'd worked out with her father to get your insurance money went off as planned."

"So you were right about thinking that most of this was aimed at me in the first place."

Ray nodded. "That was the most twisted part of her logic, that none of the acts she committed were really murders because the intended victim didn't die right away, or by her hand. Even poisoning her father was a mistake, because you never drank the tea that was supposed to make you ill on the way home from the care center, and it was her grandmother that gave it to Dennis. So of course his darling daughter had nothing to do with it."

There were still things that bothered me. "What about Edna? Do you think she committed suicide with an assist from her granddaughter?"

"Not a chance. That was definitely another murder, whether Becca sees it that way or not. The medical examiner's office called me while I was on the way from the mortuary to the church with some important lab results from the autopsy. That was the other reason I was late. Did you know that your mother-in-law was a diabetic?"

"No. But it explains why she was so strict about not letting sweets in the house. I would have been a lot more tolerant of her wishes if I'd known there was a medical reason. But what does that have to do with how she died?"

"Mrs. Peete was the kind of diabetic that didn't need insulin, but controlled her diabetes with oral medication and diet. Apparently Becca found some way to tamper with her grandmother's food and medication. She kept Edna more and more confused for a week, until the old lady was so ill she couldn't fight back. Then I'm guessing that Becca drove the car to Rancho Conejo and staged the whole suicide, and almost managed two more convenient murders to go with it."

"Can you prove any of that yet?" Even as I asked, there was something nagging the sore reaches of my brain, telling me I knew something that could help.

"Not totally. Becca and her grandmother were alone at the apartment most of the time, because the husband, Brandon, was off working at some kind of extreme sports tournament."

"He skateboards. That's why the baby's named Ollie," I added.

Ray gave me another look that said he thought my head injury was coming into play again. "Okay. I just thought somebody was an old movie fan. You know, Laurel and Hardy? Anyways, I can theorize how all of this happened, but have precious little evidence to back it up. Becca was pretty meticulous in not leaving much behind."

I rested my aching head back on the pillow again, trying to remember what was nagging me. It was something Becca had said while she was ransacking the house, talking freely to me because she didn't expect me to be able to tell anybody what she'd said. Then it came to me and I sat up. "She took a cab back to Sherman Oaks. I don't know where she caught it, probably somewhere not too near the house but within walking distance."

"How do you know this?" Ray sounded very hopeful.

"She told me. While she was ransacking the house to make it look like a burglary had taken place she found cash in Edna's pantry. She said that it almost covered the cab ride back to Sherman Oaks." I lay back again, feeling drained.

"This could be the one break I need. There can't be that many overnight cab drivers in Rancho Conejo. And there will be even less who took a fare all the way to the Valley." He grasped my hands and looked straight into my eyes. "I still wish you hadn't gone in there and gotten yourself in trouble, Gracie Lee, but since you did I'm glad you could pass on that one piece of information. Now try and get some rest, okay? I'll be back in a day or two to take a full formal statement."

"That's fine. I don't expect to be here then."

"No, I guess not. I hope you're not going back to that house, either."

I shook my head. It still didn't feel great when I did that, but at least it didn't feel like my head was ready to explode, which was a start. "Only to pack up my own things and move them over to the apartment on the Morgans' property. That's going to be home for a while."

We said goodbye and I must have dozed for a while. I couldn't go into a real deep sleep, because no one would let me. Every time I came close, it seemed someone from the nursing staff was there to jog me awake again. More than once in the course of the evening and on into daylight the next morning I reminded myself that I never wanted another concussion. They were absolutely no fun.

In those long hours, I spent a lot of time wondering what might have happened if I hadn't run into Linnette in the bookstore, or she hadn't pointed me in the direction of the Christian Friends group. Without all that, Dennis might still be alive. I could still be squabbling with Edna, and wondering where my money would turn up, if it ever did.

The more I thought about it, though, the more I knew that even if I hadn't found the Christian Friends, Becca would probably have found a way to cause most of the trouble she'd started by running my car off the embankment last August. She'd made such a series of incredibly bad choices that nothing I could have done, or not done, would have changed the outcome of what she'd done.

I had to believe that God had a purpose in my life, and part of that purpose led me to the Christian Friends. The God I believed in didn't cause the deaths of innocent people, but He didn't protect any of us from the worst of our choices, either. And sometimes those bad choices destroyed other lives, as well as our own. In this case I felt like Dennis's own bad choices in bilking so many of the people around him just led to his daughter's behavior, as well. If all she'd seen from him for over twenty years was that lying, cheating and stealing was okay, then making money off killing me for my insurance wasn't that far a stretch.

It gave me chills all over again to remember that she wasn't the one who'd taken out the policies. Dennis had arranged all that. If things had worked out in his favor, I'd be dead now and he could easily have gotten the money from his mother, making him a quarter million dollars richer, with Becca no doubt getting a share of that money, as well.

Before I had time to dwell on that any longer I got company. Linnette walked into my room, looking flushed and in a hurry. "I really intended to get here before this to come and sit with you, but something came up. Several things came up, actually." She sat down in the bedside chair.

"I didn't expect anybody to visit besides Ray. The police I expected. But I figured the rest of you had plenty to do at church on Sunday morning."

"We just got more to do. Heather's in labor. Dot and I took one look at her after early services and told her to go to the hospital."

"Wow. Did you end up calling another ambulance?"

"Not this time. Sandy had taken her to church, and had some suspicions herself. In fact she's downstairs in the labor and delivery suites with Heather now. Sandy gets a chance to get some mothering points here as her daughter's labor coach. After everything that has gone on, I'm surprised Heather wants her, but she does."

"As far as anybody knows, is she okay?"

"Too soon to tell. But I sort of thought yesterday when I saw her at the luncheon that this might be happening. The girl was so grouchy and antsy at the same time."

I was glad to hear somebody else had noticed the same thing I had. At least all of my perceptions yesterday weren't flawed.

"Thanks for coming to tell me."

Linnette smiled. "I didn't come just to tell you that. I came to spring you out of here if I can. Figured you'd need a ride home, and I suspect they'll be discharging you soon."

"Probably before noon. At least that's what the nurses have said. I got to eat breakfast and I didn't throw up or anything, so I should be good to go." I got teary again.

"But go where, is that what you're thinking?" Linnette's voice was gentle.

"I know where I belong, it's just a case of how I'm going to get there," I told her. Moving all that stuff sounded pretty daunting right now.

As usual, Linnette was a step ahead of me. "Don't worry about it. Dot and I already talked about that. We'll help you pack up the basics from Edna's house, including your computer and all of your school stuff and most of your clothes, and take it over to the apartment. We decided that you shouldn't spend another night in that house, Gracie Lee."

I couldn't agree with her more. After everything that had happened there, it was the last place I wanted to be. "Thanks. You all are the best."

Linnette waved me off. "Save the compliments for Wednesday night at Christian Friends when we do affirmations. We're going to get through an entire real, structured meeting this week if we have to stay until midnight."

* * *

Wednesday night the coffee was hot, the people were friendly and there wasn't a chocolate-chip cookie in sight, in my honor—just peanut butter and oatmeal raisin—and some brownies. The meeting started off with all the official Christian Friends stuff, good prayers and a dandy devotion. Like Linnette had said, she was doing it all by the book this time.

Once they worked their way around to me I had plenty to tell them, although they were less interested in the fact that I'd started my new job at the Coffee Corner or that Ray had taken a formal statement from me on Tuesday than they were in solving Dennis's murder. I told everyone what I could; there were plenty of details that would have to wait until either a grand jury hearing or eventually a trial was held for Becca.

"I have one question I imagine you can answer," Dot said with a smile. "Even though you've been in that apartment behind my house for days now, you haven't ever told me what Ben's good news was when he was trying to reach you Saturday afternoon."

"It's very good news," I said, not resisting a motherly grin. "My brilliant son is going to be joining me at Pacific Oaks in the fall. He's been offered nearly a full-ride scholarship. Only his books, parking and spending money are going to fall to us."

Apparently he'd gotten one of those "fat envelopes" that high school seniors everywhere look for in the late fall and early spring. I was thrilled, not only because he'd be that close to me all the time, but that it came when it did. If Pacific Oaks had waited even one extra day to send his admissions packet, Becca might have gotten away with another murder.

"What does he think of going to the same school as Mom, and at the same time?" Lexy asked.

"He's happy to be coming out here, and we won't see each other that much, I suspect. Freshmen and second-year grad students have very little in common. His scholarship will include housing on campus, so he won't be living with me much."

"Still, it would be a good thing to get that extra bathroom added on to the apartment," Dot said. "I wonder if we could get it done before school ends in June."

"Don't hold your breath on it," I told her. "Missouri schools end a lot earlier than the ones out here. I could be going out for his graduation right before Memorial Day." It was good to think about that—about moving forward, and late spring in Missouri with all the flowers blooming and all these warm, pleasant positive things to focus on. It had been quite a while since I had a bunch of positive things to look forward to at the same time.

Now it seemed like almost everything I was looking forward to was positive. And to underscore that, before I could say anything else, Heather came into the room carrying a baby seat full of the cutest little squirt possible. "Everybody, this is Corinna Grace," she said, pulling aside a pink flowered blanket to reveal an adorable, scrunched-up pink face. "Not only is she beautiful, she scored a nearly perfect nine-point-five on the Apgar scale." Mom beamed and baby yawned, making all of us laugh and coo and crowd around.

"Pretty name," Paula said, stroking the baby's soft cheek. "Where does it come from?"

"The Corinna part from one of my grandmothers," Heather said, smiling down at her bundle of joy. "And the Grace is for all of you, in a funny sort of way. I mean, it's only by God's grace that she's here, and I was here to have her and everything turned out as well as it did. For me, at least, the Christian Friends are the best example of God's grace I've ever seen."

"Amen to that one," Dot said with conviction. "Now how about one of us getting you a big glass of ice water and a couple of those cookies and you spend your group time telling us all the gory details of your labor and delivery that nobody else wants to hear."

The group laughed as one, and I was struck again by how wonderful it was to have this group of women in my life. Heather was right; it *was* only God's grace that had led both of us here, and to this place where we could sit in the same room and I could listen to her launch in on this fascinating tale of new life in all its messy glory.

Life is like that, even when we aren't giving birth. It is messy and glorious and awful all at the same time and God is always there to walk with us if we let Him. And sometimes, when we're the most fortunate, He sends people like this to walk alongside us and remind us that we're not alone.

The last thing I felt this night was alone. I poured myself another cup of coffee and listened to Heather while Corinna slept beside her. "So anyway, my back was killing me, and you two were right, I needed to go to the hospital, because when I got out of Mom's car at Los Robles, the seat was all wet."

"Your water broke!" came the chorus, which I joined. Several of us were shaking our heads in remembrance of similar events.

"You should have put a beach towel under you, sweetie," Linnette said.

"I know that *now*. Not that it's any help for Mom's upholstery." We all groaned in response, too many of us having been there ourselves. I felt like part of the women's tribe, sitting around the campfire. These were my sisters in Christ and it felt very, very good to be home.

For now, California is home. There was too much keeping me here to think about going back to Missouri, except for visits. It's still new and confusing out here on the Left Coast with all its quirks, but some things are the same or even better. God's love still surrounds me in this place where I can wear black rubber sandals in February and not have frostbite. And that is an awesome thing.

* * * * *

DISCUSSION QUESTIONS FOR *LOVE THE SINNER*

1. Gracie Lee discovers a terrible secret about her husband. Have you ever known anyone who discovered a troubling secret about their spouse? How did they deal with it?

2. When did you begin to suspect the killer? Did you go back and reread to see if you could find hints about the killer's identity?

3. How does the author contrast between the three women who have been married to, or involved with, Dennis Peete? What is it about their lives that has made them the way they are?

4. Have you ever heard of a support group like the Christian Friends described in this book? If you were part of such a group, what would you change about the one described here? What would you keep the same?

5. When Linnette invites Gracie Lee to be part of the Christian Friends, she expresses her concern first, then brings her into the group, shares Scripture with her in the form of the Psalms, and only after all that does she invite her to church. Why do you think she took that approach? Do you think her approach was valid?

6. With whom do you most identify in this book? Why?

7. Detective Fernandez can't seem to understand Gracie Lee's capacity to forgive Heather. How could you explain the Christian nature of forgiveness to someone who isn't familiar with Scripture and doesn't go to church? What language could you use?

8. There are a lot of women involved in this story—Gracie Lee, the Christian Friends, Edna. How do you think this story would be different if there were more men involved?

9. The parent/child relationship is shown in many forms—Gracie Lee and Ben, Edna and Dennis, Dennis and Becca, Becca and her mother, Heather and her mother. What communication issues do you see among the relationships? What could be done in their relationships to improve communication?

10. In the front of this book is the following Bible verses: *Ephesians* 2:8-9 "For it is by grace you have been saved, through faith—and this is not from yourselves, it is the gift of God—not by works, so that no one can boast." Where is God's grace most evident in Gracie Lee's life?

He offered her the opportunity to give her baby a life of privilege, instead of the abject poverty Mara Rosemond remembered from her own childhood. But at what cost?

"Catherine Palmer... understands hurts as well as joys, and portrays them authentically and insightfully."
—Randy Alcorn, bestselling author of *Deadline*

Love's Haven
by Catherine Palmer

Available in stores May 2005.

Visit your local bookseller.

Steeple Hill®

www.SteepleHill.com   SHCP538TR

It was a story to put Hideaway, Missouri,
in the national headlines...

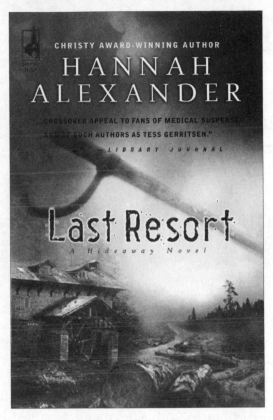

A missing child...
A woman in crisis...
A man of faith...

Don't miss this next exciting
novel in the Hideaway series.

In stores June 2005.
Visit your local bookseller.

Steeple
Hill®

www.SteepleHill.com   SHHA540TR

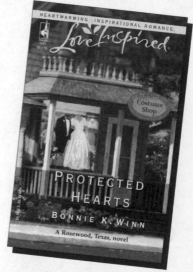

Love Inspired

PROTECTED HEARTS

BY

BONNIE K. WINN

When her husband and child were murdered,
Emma Perry lost her faith—and her identity. Then
she started a new life in Rosewood, Texas, where the
caring community helped her regain her faith and
introduced her to Seth McAllister, her embittered
neighbor who was also struggling to overcome a
tragedy. Together, Seth and Emma began to open
their hearts to love, just as the still-obsessed killer
picks up Emma's trail....

Don't miss PROTECTED HEARTS
On sale May 2005

Available at your favorite retail outlet.

www.SteepleHill.com   LIPHBKWTR

Love Inspired®

ANOTHER HEARTWARMING STORY OF

Men of Praise

HEARTS IN HARMONY

BY

GAIL SATTLER

Adrian Braithwaite was thrilled with the
newest member of the church's worship team:
Celeste Hackett was a talented pianist and a lovely
lady. Yet there was more to Celeste than her beauty.
She was hiding a secret. And when a threat from her
rocky past arrived, Adrian realized he wanted to
protect his musical partner...and future wife.

**Men of Praise: Faithful and strong,
these men lead in worship and love.**

Don't miss HEARTS IN HARMONY
On sale May 2005

Available at your favorite retail outlet.

www.SteepleHill.com   LIHIHGSTR

Love Inspired®

Journey to Forever

by

Carol Steward

An eight-day road trip with notorious radio
personality Colin Wright wasn't something
fledgling journalist Nikki Post was looking forward
to. Yet the Colin she met wasn't the immature
prankster she'd been expecting. But when trouble
threatened to end the trip, would Nikki's newfound
role in Colin's life end…or continue forever?

Don't miss JOURNEY TO FOREVER
On sale May 2005

Available at your favorite retail outlet.

www.SteepleHill.com   LIJTFCSTR

A SHELTERING LOVE

BY

TERRI REED

Claire Wilcox sensed there was more to Nick Andrews
than met the eye. The handsome stranger who'd
saved her life twice was running from something.
Claire knew all about running—she'd been a runaway
herself. As Nick helped Claire repair the damages to
the teen center she'd established, he found himself
longing to forge a relationship with Claire...and
the God he'd shut out of his heart.

Don't miss A SHELTERING LOVE
On sale May 2005

Available at your favorite retail outlet.

www.SteepleHill.com   LIASLTRTR